A SECRET GARDEN REMIX

# THE REMIXED CLASSICS SERIES

*A Clash of Steel: A Treasure Island Remix*
by **C.B. Lee**

*So Many Beginnings: A Little Women Remix*
by **Bethany C. Morrow**

*Travelers Along the Way: A Robin Hood Remix*
by **Aminah Mae Safi**

*What Souls Are Made Of: A Wuthering Heights Remix*
by **Tasha Suri**

*Self-Made Boys: A Great Gatsby Remix*
by **Anna-Marie McLemore**

*My Dear Henry: A Jekyll & Hyde Remix*
by **Kalynn Bayron**

*Teach the Torches to Burn: A Romeo & Juliet Remix*
by **Caleb Roehrig**

*Into the Bright Open: A Secret Garden Remix*
by **Cherie Dimaline**

*Most Ardently: A Pride & Prejudice Remix*
by **Gabe Cole Novoa**

# INTO THE BRIGHT OPEN

## A Secret Garden Remix

CHERIE DIMALINE

FEIWEL AND FRIENDS
New York

A Feiwel and Friends Book
An imprint of Macmillan Publishing Group, LLC
120 Broadway, New York, NY 10271 • fiercereads.com





Library of Congress Cataloging-in-Publication Data

Names: Dimaline, Cherie, 1975– author. | Burnett, Frances Hodgson, 1849–1924. Secret garden.
Title: Into the bright open : a Secret garden remix / Cherie Dimaline.
Description: First edition. | New York : Feiwel & Friends, 2023. | Series: Remixed classics ; [8] | Audience: Ages 13 and up. | Audience: Grades 10–12. | Summary: In this queer reimagining of The secret garden, fifteen-year-old orphan Mary sets off to live in the Georgian Bay wilds where she discovers family secrets both wonderful and horrifying.
Identifiers: LCCN 2022061544 | ISBN 9781250842657 (hardcover)
Subjects: CYAC: Orphans—Fiction. | Secrets—Fiction. | Cousins—Fiction. | Gardens—Fiction. | Friendship—Fiction. | LGBTQ+ people—Fiction. | Canada—History—20th century—Fiction. | LCGFT: Historical fiction. | Novels.
Classification: LCC PZ7.1.D5638 In 2023 | DDC [Fic]—dc23
LC record available at https://lccn.loc.gov/2022061544

First edition, 2023
Book design by Samira Iravani
Feiwel and Friends logo designed by Filomena Tuosto
Printed in the United States of America

ISBN 978-1-250-84265-7
1 3 5 7 9 10 8 6 4 2

*For my Georgian Bay Grandmothers—Edna, Henrietta (Hattie), Philomene, Sophie, Cecile, Olive, Angelique, Francoise, and more.*

*And especially for my mother, Joanie.*

# 1

# Death Knocks and the Journey Begins

Mary Craven didn't think about death until the day it knocked politely on her bedroom door and invited itself in. That, she decided soon after, was the perfect way to describe death—something that pretends to act on formalities like knocking but then, in the end, does exactly what it wants to do.

In this instance, death came in the guise of her nanny, Miss Patricks, who was the one rapping at the door, then scuttling inside with her chin trembling. She was bringing the news that would change Mary's life forever.

"I'm afraid there's been an awful accident, my dear," she managed through a throat full of sobs. She hung her gray head so that her jowls grazed her ample chest, moving the pocket watch she had pinned there to-and-fro. "An awful, terrible accident."

She was wringing an embroidered handkerchief to ribbons in her hands. This annoyed Mary, who despised useless fidgeting and stalling. In fact, if it were not obvious the woman would break down at the slightest provocation, she would have yelled at her. Instead, she sighed, opening her green eyes wider in an expectant expression.

"It's your parents, my dear. Your lovely parents . . ."

These were words she hadn't heard before—her parents, *lovely*? There were many things that could be said about her parents, but *lovely* was not one of them. Something was amiss. Mary had the feeling now of running out of breath when one was in the lake—those seconds before the burn started and you felt you must fight for your life, just before you found the bottom and kicked to the surface.

"What of my parents?" Mary said, wanting to get to the end of this encounter as soon as possible.

"I'm afraid, sweet child . . . they have passed on."

There were words after those, but none of them mattered. They blended into a kind of low-pitched ringing in her ears.

"Leave me." Mary said it without hearing her own words, her eyes caught now by a gray bird that had settled on her window ledge. "Leave me now."

She assumed Miss Patricks toddled her way out at some

point. But she couldn't be sure, because she ceased to notice anything around her except for that bird.

Her mother had a dress that color. She'd worn it last week when the City Council came for dinner. Her father, also a councilman, with his impressive mustache and impressive rounded gut, was a man with power in Toronto. Her mother, always removed from her daughter as if surrounded by her own light, was considered by society to be a great beauty. For both these reasons, fancy dinner parties happened all the time at their house. And that evening Mary had been sent away just before dinner to eat soup and crackers in her suite under the supervision of Miss Patricks, even though she was far too old to still have a nanny and just old enough to be a guest at a dinner party.

She had noticed her mother's dress before being banished. It was silk and lace with tailored hems at her feet and severe shoulders that did nothing to hide her enviable figure. The color made her eyes seem violet and more alive than usual. Mary wanted to tell her how magical she looked, with her hair pulled up in an intricate knot and left curly at her temples, her earlobes decorated with bright pearls. She wanted to tell her how she was proud to have such a beautiful woman as her mother. But she didn't. It was her small punishment for being sent away. Cecile Craven would have to go down to dinner without any compliment whatsoever.

"I think Mother looks awful tonight," she told Miss Patricks around a mouthful of lukewarm tomato puree. "Like she's in mourning."

Miss Patricks was shocked, though she shouldn't have been. She had been Mary's nanny since the beginning and was well accustomed to her moods. "Miss Mary, what an untrue and unkind thing to say!"

"She looks like she could leave straight from dessert to the funeral home."

Mary wondered, watching as the bird took flight, if that's where her mother was now, and if that was the dress she was wearing.

No one came to put her to bed. She was fifteen—the occasion had been marked by a small dinner her father couldn't make time for—so she didn't really need any assistance. But she liked to stay up late and read, and it usually fell to someone else to remind her to put the books away and get to sleep. It was a part of her routine. In fact, some nights she stayed up longer than she wanted to, her eyes watering, her brain refusing to hold the sentences longer than it took to reach the end of one. Still she would remain propped up against her pillows, waiting for the door to open and the admonishing to start.

But tonight the sky grew heavy and the moon pulled itself high, and no one came to remind her of anything.

The night bugs tuned their instruments and set into an orchestral swell, and still no one came.

Everything was dark, outside and in. Mary hadn't eaten anything since lunch. She stayed seated at her small table by the window, wondering if this was how it would be from now on—if no one would ever come for her again.

Later as she slumped over the table, sleeping on her folded arms so that her cheek would be crisscrossed with indents, she was roused and put under her covers fully clothed. Only her shoes were unlaced and removed. In the morning she found those shoes sitting on her chair.

*What an odd place to put shoes*, she thought. She knew whoever had put her to bed last night had not been Miss Patricks, who would have insisted on taking off her dress and pinafore and sliding a crisp white nightie over her head. At the very least, she would have carried her shoes to the closet. It must have been one of the other servants—perhaps her mother's maid, Isabelle, or her father's valet, George. She thought they must be wandering the halls at this hour like stiff-shirted ghosts, with no one to wait on.

For the next few days, she was left largely on her own. She walked the hallways of the house and through the manicured lawns. Every now and again, Miss Patricks would call her in for some under-spiced food and once made her a bath, but even the nanny seemed to be there only part-time. Mary began to wonder if she was left alone at night, so she climbed down the stairs past dark and found Miss Patricks and Isabelle drinking her father's whiskey from her mother's good china.

Mary wanted to yell at them, to reprimand them for being thieves and lazy to boot, but she couldn't find her voice these days. Instead, she threw the book she was carrying—*Kim* by Rudyard Kipling—over the banister of the curved stairs. It landed with a resounding *thump* in the foyer and scared the women so badly, Isabelle spilled whiskey on her apron.

It was an odd thing to be completely alone, without ally or friend. If she had had siblings, she supposed this was when they would have rallied together. She had once hidden in the hallway while her mother had tea with her friends. One woman explained how a wife could take charge of her life and take certain precautions to ensure the number of children she bore was limited. Mary's mother shared that she was happy to have gotten what was required of her out of the way so she could live her life. Mary understood that she was that which had been "gotten out of the way."

She wondered if she had been a prettier child, a more agreeable child, that perhaps there would have been more children in the house. She carried that burden, layering it with spite and aloofness until it no longer cut, like a grain of sand polished inside an oyster.

The funeral was just as her mother would have wanted it—full of society's best and brightest fawning over her heavy-framed portrait. And it was also exactly as her father would have wanted it—stuffed with the most powerful men in Toronto, all taking the opportunity of being in the same room to discuss business.

During the service, the minister talked about how John and Cecile Craven were the perfect couple, the epitome of their time, how the new century could use more good people like them. "They made it into 1900, but left us too soon for this new age to properly benefit from their like."

Even Mary thought that was a bit much. All her father did was take meetings and talk until the other men had to stifle yawns. All her mother did was drink wine before lunch and throw parties where she could surround herself with the other diminished women with their soft hands and sharp words. She thought the minister was a bad preacher and a worse poet, but she held her tongue, squished in between the mayor and her nanny in the first pew. Miss Patricks was beside herself to have such a place of honor. Mary noticed the mayor smelled like tobacco and mothballs and had too much hair in his ears.

She couldn't help but hear the way people were speaking about her—*Poor child*, and *Little wretch*, and *Such a pity she wasn't a few years older, she could be married off quick enough*. All this and yet no one bothered to speak *to* her. It was horrible, but she remained unmoved. In fact, besides the flash of anger at the servants drinking her father's whiskey, Mary was unmoved for most of those days.

Until, of course, she was bundled onto a carriage and taken north.

Miss Patricks was the one who packed her things, prattling on as she did. Perhaps she expected the girl to release her legendary temper. When Mary remained tight-lipped after they had boarded and started off, the nanny sighed deeply and took out her knitting. No more effort at conversation was made.

It had been an hour, and the houses and roads of the city were long gone when Mary suddenly began to speak. It was as if the city itself had been holding her silent. Now that they were out in the wild open, her thoughts were loosened and her voice followed.

"What will become of the house?"

Mary wasn't sentimental. She learned that word from a book a few years back and tried to figure out how it fit in her life. Turns out, it didn't. She didn't hold on to any of her old dolls—instead she'd asked George to take them to the orphanage or the dump, either one was fine. She didn't have a favorite dress or a good-luck locket. She didn't even have any friends, not really. But suddenly, she felt unmoored. Her hands felt too empty. She felt like she was missing something, or maybe even someone.

Miss Patricks, on the verge of napping, gave a start, snorting as she did.

"Oh, well, the house was appointed to your father along

with his position," she replied. "I would imagine the city takes it back."

"And their things?"

Miss Patricks, seemingly offended that the next question should be about baubles and furniture and not her, answered without cushion. "Auctioned off. Already in process. Of course, the proceeds will be put into a trust for you along with the inheritance."

Mary greeted this new knowledge with silence. But, roused now—upset, even—Miss Patricks rambled on.

"And that's all well and good but what of the staff? Not so much as a pension or a reference letter. I suppose I might as well head back down east. There's nothing here. God knows your guardian didn't extend the invitation to me. Me, the one person who raised the girl, for God's sake."

Mary was suddenly interested. "They say I am to live with my uncle Craven, but I don't know him. Is he a man of wealth?"

The older woman shook her head. "I know that you were raised in a rather cold home, but that you, at your age, are even concerned with a man's standing is an odd thing. And that your first questions are not about his goodwill or his household, his willingness to take you in blood or not, well, that's just unseemly."

Miss Patricks adjusted her sweater, her thin lips pursed. But she couldn't stop there—she clearly wanted to gossip about the mysterious Mr. William Craven. "And yes, to answer your question. He is very successful. But he is also an odd character. Never even bothered to come down to the city. Just stayed up here in this godforsaken wilderness. They say the entire settlement is nothing but Indian French half-breeds who've forgotten their paler roots. Imagine that, preferring their company? Doesn't say much about a person, if you ask me."

Mary was sorry she had begun this conversation already. She remembered her mother saying it was important to remind staff they were employees. That if you gave them an inch, they'd be asking and giving advice. Mary knew her mother was not a very good example as far as parents went, but she was still the only example she had. So she sat up straighter and let her eyes glaze over. "I didn't."

"You didn't what, dear?"

"I didn't ask you."

The rest of the trip was carried out in silence.

# 2

# The Manor on the Bay

The journey was long and bumpy. There were wide roads, but some parts were less used than others, and the going got rough. The trees on either side were dense, and more than once she saw a deer skulking at the edges.

When they got closer to their destination, there were more carriages on the road, some hauling wagons stacked with giant logs and smaller cut planks. They drove by a family on one corner, dressed in patched trousers tied with bright sashes, who were selling baskets and jars of canned fruit.

"Humph, already with the Indians," Miss Patricks scoffed.

Mary was more interested because of her nanny's disdain.

She leaned out the window and locked eyes with the tallest girl, whose dark hair hung to her waist. There was something about her eyes, the way they connected with her own without any shame, that made Mary envious. She pulled herself back into her carriage and refused to look outside at the small wooden houses and long horses ridden by men who tipped their hats or looked in with interest.

The carriage turned onto a curved road. The trees here were white birch and calloused oak. Mary leaned her head against the wall and counted the turns as they took them. She was feeling nauseous. Not from the travel, but from something she didn't want to name—a thing akin to fear that made her want to sleep. But there was no time for that now. The carriage came to a stop and shook as the driver climbed down from his perch.

They were met at the front gate by a young woman in a green cloak. She was tall and thin and had the most beautiful hair Mary had ever seen, all wrapped about her head in thick braids like a kind of hat.

"I suppose this is my replacement then," Miss Patricks sniffed. "Looks to be not much older than her charge."

Trunks and suitcases were unloaded as the woman came over to greet them. "You must be Mary. Me, I'm Flora. Pleased to meet you." The girl was cheerful and brimming with an energy that shocked the travel-weary newcomers. "And Miss Patricks, then?"

The older woman did not shake the girl's hand. Instead, she looked away and sniffed again, then directed her unease to the men lifting down trunks. "You there, be careful with those. If you can't do it right just leave it and I'll manage it myself, but don't expect any extra if that's to be the case."

Flora leaned down. "Well," she whispered conspiratorially in Mary's ear. "She's a bear, no? Must have been a real fight for you, trying to breathe around that one all these years."

Mary was enchanted by the young woman's voice. It was free and smooth, not stuffy like the British immigrants her father entertained in his office, which apparently meant smoking cigars and grumbling loudly. And she spoke to Mary like she was grown—which of course, she was, though no one else seemed to notice. There was an ease about her, something unseen in any household staff Mary had ever encountered.

"Um, that's a huge lot of baggage for one girl here," Flora noted.

"Well, there are my cases among them, since I will be staying a while to get her settled in before moving on," Miss Patricks answered, still not meeting the new girl's gaze. "I always said it takes a proper lady to raise one, and leaving her here with nothing but trees and Indians? Well, that decision was out of my hands." She raised her hands to demonstrate her point. "The least I can do, out of Christian charity, is to make sure there is a smooth transition."

Flora squinted her eyes at the woman. "Then you'll be glad to know I'm taking over right this moment, so you don't have to stay, madam." She clapped her hands with false cheer. "The men have been told to drive you straight back to Toronto. You know, so you don't have to stay here with the likes of me. Happy news for you."

There were wide eyes all around. The carriage driver chuckled behind his leather glove.

"I mean, we wouldn't want any of your great ladyshipness to rub off on the wilderness and leave you wanting." Flora was being snide, but she did it with confidence and a big smile, so there was no way to know quite how to respond. She waved her hand toward the carriage and called out, "Men, you can leave the young lady's belongings just here then, at the gate. I'll send for them. And Miss Patricks, you can say your goodbyes now. Mary, I'll be just over here, then we'll walk up to the manor together."

And with that, she lifted her skirts and walked over to the tall iron fence to wait.

Their goodbyes were short—Miss Patricks was too stunned by Flora's reprimand to say much more than to remind Mary to be good and warn her to not pick up on "the new girl's atrocious grammar, though what could be expected from her kind." For her part, Mary was glad to see her nanny go—she may have not been a sentimental being, but there was also something satisfying about severing those last links to her parents' deaths and her own childhood at the same time, in the same body. Watching Miss Patricks be carried away, she felt light.

"I see you're not one for crying, then," Flora remarked, pushing open the gate and starting down the drive.

"Not really," Mary responded. "Makes my head ache and doesn't do anything to lift my mood anyway."

"Truer words have never been spoken. A useless thing, that," Flora agreed. She shocked Mary by linking arms with her and walking like that up the lane. Mary wasn't used to physicality of any kind. She walked very carefully, not sure of how to proceed. But she would commit to whatever odd customs she was to encounter. She assumed this was one of them, this casual closeness with staff.

"Me? I am a crier, mon dieu, yes. Just can't seem to stop it from happening, and then once it starts, it's hard for me to turn it off," Flora said. "Anyway, welcome to your new home where I am sure there will be no need to cry at all, for either of us."

The house rose in front of them, taller and more ornate than any Mary had seen since leaving the city. Once, it must have been a cheerful blue, the wood all painted the same hue except for the white trimming around the windows and wide porch. But now it was a kind of somber gray. Mary thought she liked it better this way—she preferred serious houses. A house needed to keep you safe, keep things out. Already the place had far too much gingerbreading and too many windows for her taste. But at least it was serious in tone.

"The Craven Manor is the biggest home on the Georgian Bay," Flora told her. "It took ten years to build and has over forty rooms. My dad was one of the men who worked on it. Says a whole forest went into it, squirrels and all."

"I've seen bigger," Mary sniffed, though she wasn't sure she had. "Back in Toronto."

Flora did not let the small jab puncture her good humor. "Oh, I'm sure there were loads of great things in the city." She called out to an older man who was meticulously trimming the cedar bushes into rounded nubs. "Jean, the mademoiselle's trunks are at the gate. Can you take the wagon and pick them up there?"

He didn't answer. Instead, he placed the tree clippers on the ground and started around the house, wiping his forehead with an old rag as he walked.

"Jean doesn't talk much, but he's as good as they come, I can tell you that as fact," Flora said, pulling Mary up the steps. "For now, I'll take you to your quarters. I'm afraid Mr. Craven is out on a voyage, so it'll just be us. Us would be me, you, Jean, and Hippolyte, who mostly takes care of Mr. Craven when he's home. Oh, and Philomene in the kitchen. And . . ." She paused and then jumped to the next sentiment. "Anyway, it's a real small family, but we make do."

Family? Mary had never been in a place where the servants considered themselves family. Oddly, it made her feel happy about this place, to know there was a real family living inside. She imagined them gathering for dinner at a great table and tending the garden in matching coats and gloves.

The foyer was dark and flanked by a winding staircase that split into two separate wings of the house above. A dozen doors ran along both walls, all closed, which made Mary curious to peek in each one. This was her favorite game at her own house—her *old house*, she reminded herself—to "discover" new areas that she was told were off-limits.

One such room had been her mother's. Not the bedroom she shared with her father, but the room just down from the master suite; a small haven where she kept all her clothes lined up against the walls—gowns beside everyday dresses, off-season coats and pretty nightgowns hanging alongside one another like odd couples. Along the floor, like obedient soldiers ready for battle, were her mother's shoes, polished and lined up neatly. But Mary's favorite thing about it was the curved vanity table set in the center of it all, flanked by a low, velvet seat. It was exactly what she imagined a dressing room would be in a Broadway theater. Her mother had even had a large droopy crystal chandelier hung directly overhead. And on the shiny mahogany surface lay every imaginable bauble and jar to make one beautiful. There were a dozen perfume bottles, metal tubes of creamy lipsticks in every color, and costume jewelry tangled in and among the powders, puffs, and bobby pins.

Suddenly Mary was curious. "Do I have an aunt?"

Flora's forehead wrinkled a bit. "Of course. Mrs. Craven is out for the weekend at her sister's."

Mary stopped in front of a portrait. In it sat a beautiful woman in a red dress, her dark hair shiny and hanging loose, her teeth showing white in a full smile. Mary had never seen a portrait with a real smile. She just assumed it was forbidden. Her own mother had a somber portrait done, one that seemed to be specially made for her funeral, where it stood on an ornate easel by a massive floral arrangement. "Is this her?"

"Oh dear, no." Flora sighed. "That would be the former Missus Craven—Hattie. She was a Trudeau before a Craven, her. She passed on about fourteen years now. I never met her, but my mother knew her well. Says she was lovely, her. One of the best dancers in the county."

"She was a dancer? Like on Broadway?" Mary asked, her mother's vanity still fresh in her mind.

"Ha! Lord, no. In the community. They say she jigged fast enough to break the ground to dirt and danced till the dust was clouds at her knees."

"Community?" Mary was confused as ever, but there was too much to distract her right now. She wanted to see every inch of this house, to wander the grounds, to sneak behind the locked doors.

“My community. The half-breeds from the island settled here.” Flora smiled back at the painting before looking at Mary and clucking her tongue as the girl stifled a yawn. “Mon dieu,” she said. “Let’s get you to your rooms so you can rest for a while. Before you fall asleep on your feet!”

---

Mary rarely dreamt. She might have on occasion, but she never remembered so even if she did. But on that day, during her first sleep in the Craven Manor with the rush and pull of the Georgian Bay filling all the corners, she had a dream.

In it, she was on a wooden swing hanging from the low branch of the oak tree in her Toronto yard. In reality, there had been no swing in that tree, or anywhere on the property, and if there had been, Mary wouldn’t have bothered. She preferred to fill her minutes with useful things like books and planning. She planned all sorts of things—trips to the European continent, dinners she would like to learn to cook, languages she would one day speak fluently. She listed these plans in neat, orderly columns on a sheet of yellow paper kept in her desk. But in the dream, she was swinging. And she loved it.

There was something about the loss of footing that opened the door for the loss of time without regret. It made her stomach feel funny, as if it were floating under her rib cage like a helium balloon. And the wind, made by her own movement, pushed her brown curls off her face in the best way, as if they were being stroked by a careful hand.

And then suddenly, as is the way with dreams, there was a girl swinging beside her. Mary wasn't startled, but it was a surprise. It was as if the branch had grown to accommodate a second seat in the seconds when she closed her eyes to enjoy the downward swoop.

"My mother wouldn't be pleased," the girl said between giggles. "Wasting time like this."

"Mine wouldn't care," Mary replied, not feeling the sting these words should have carried. "She'd have to notice me first to notice I was wasting time."

The two of them laughed, egging each other on to push farther, stretch their toes higher.

"I'd notice you," the girl yelled from the top of her arc, right as her direction changed, and her red hair fell into her face.

"I barely notice myself, to be honest," Mary sang back.

"How is that possible?"

Mary wanted to keep her eyes shut and on the girl at the same time. She settled for watching the tops of the trees. "You just have to ignore your own thoughts, I suppose."

"No, silly," the girl cut in. "Not how does one not notice themselves in general. I mean, how could anyone not notice you in particular?"

"Why's that?"

There was a grinding noise as the girl used her black shoes to dig into the dirt and stop herself. Mary noticed the dust made little clouds by her shins. "Because you're remarkable."

Mary felt her cheeks get hot. She snapped her eyes shut tight, trying as hard as she could to ignore her own thoughts.

---

Waking up in a new house after always having woken up in the same room all the mornings of your life should have been disorientating at least, terrifying at most. Thankfully, the heavy drapes had been shut against the windows and the room was cloaked in a thin layer of darkness. So Mary had a moment to remember all the things she must.

Her parents were dead. Her nanny was gone. She was in a large house in a strange wild land owned by a relative she had never met before—her father's older brother, to be exact. These facts lined up and jumped off some dark cliff into her stomach, creating a weight that pulled at Mary's limbs so that it was hard to sit up.

Once she had that all sorted out, she took an extra moment, her hands over her stomach to keep it in place, and thought of the girl from her dream.

She knew her. Well, that's not entirely true. The girl was her neighbor, a loud redhead who often had friends over and spent hours in her gardens with her siblings—two small boys and a baby they called Stinky. Mary had watched her from her bedroom window for years.

Once, the girl had been brought over by her mother in an attempt to create a relationship between the two households.

"Just figured since we are right next door, we should be familiar. And, since our girls are the same age, thereabouts, they could become best of friends!" Mrs. McCarthy was cheerful, almost to the point of coming off as a bit simple.

Mary knew her mother would drop the "almost" part of that description, that she would find the woman absolutely daft. Added to that, Mrs. McCarthy was Irish, fresh from the homeland, and her husband was a lowly supervisor at the sugar refinery. They only lived next door in this neighborhood because Mr. McCarthy had inherited the house. Mary knew this because her mother knew this. So she knew there was no way she was about to meet her future best friend. Cecile Craven would never allow it.

"How kind," Cecile drawled. "Unfortunately, we cannot visit right now. We're on our way out. Perhaps another time."

Mrs. McCarthy was not so easily dismissed. "Oh, to be sure. We'll just step in for a moment so the wee girls can meet. Then we'll be on our way. This is Brandy."

A redheaded girl was pulled over the threshold by the hand. She had none of her mother's nervous energy but still seemed out of sorts. It was sweet how much her mother cared. It was obvious by the way she had been groomed and prepared for this moment, how much the older woman wanted to present her in her best light. For her part, Cecile tipped her head and looked up the stairs, to where Mary had stopped halfway down. That was the extent of it—an annoyed stare.

Mary came the rest of the way down, embarrassed by her mother's rudeness. They were not going anywhere—they never went anywhere together. Her embarrassment made her stiff so that she seemed reluctant. She stood in front of the girl, who was slightly shorter than her and waited for whatever came next.

The girl held out her hand. "Hello, I'm Brandy McCarthy."

"Mary Craven." She had meant to say more, to take Brandy's hand, to guide her into the sitting room where they should have been brought to begin with. She meant to offer them tea and then send Miss Patricks to make it. She meant to do the things that a girl was supposed to do to enchant another, to form a bond that would carry them through their young lives. But she seemed to be stuck fast to the hardwood floor.

She wanted nothing more than to take the girl's hand. And why not, if it was being offered? She imagined her skin would be warm but dry, that she would have strength in her fingers, that her fingers would slide in between Mary's own and they would be joined, then and there.

Brandy McCarthy had the brightest eyes she'd ever seen. They were greener than the ivy that clung to her windowpane.

And her skin was dusted with small, dark freckles that carried down her neck and over the back of her outstretched hand, as if something soft had exploded nearby and covered her in its fragments. Mary felt her breath circling in her chest and had to will it into an exhale.

"Well, we'll be sure to send word when a visit would be more appropriate," Cecile cut in. "Mary, say goodbye to our neighbors."

She made sure to use the title that gave them the most distance—not new friends, certainly not guests, since they had arrived uninvited, but simply who they were based on a mere circumstance of geography.

Later that afternoon, sitting at her open window while writing out a plan for how she was going to woo Brandy into a lifelong friendship (*Meet for tea; ask Miss Patricks to escort us into the city for shopping; build a gate in the fence between our yards . . .*), Mary heard Brandy telling her brothers about the visit.

"It was so cold in there my arse almost dropped off. Like a witch's cave. And the girl? She was awful. The snobbiest snot ever to live."

Mary closed the drapes and crumpled up her plan. She threw herself on her bed to read a book instead. *Who needed friends anyway?*

And now Brandy McCarthy was in her dreams.

"Am I so alone that a stranger plays the part of companion?" she asked out loud.

This wasn't something she did often, speaking to no one but herself. In Toronto, Miss Patricks had slept in the next room. She would pop over if Mary so much as coughed. She knew a part of her was just testing the limits of her privacy in this new house. She watched the door, but it stayed shut. And even though she was glad for the freedom to hold conversations with herself, she unexpectedly felt lonesome.

And then there was a noise. It was distant and wild, like a hummingbird buzzing around the far reaches of her hearing.

"What's that?" Apparently, she was someone who talked to themselves regularly now.

She closed her eyes and leaned into the sound. It almost sounded like . . . someone crying?

Mary got up, crept to the door, and opened it. She poked her head out into the hall and tried to discern which direction the sound was coming from. Out here, it seemed to be coming from the walls, as if it had soaked into the wainscoting and was leaking down through the floorboards.

"Oh good, you're up." Flora wiped her hands on a small apron tied at her waist. "I was just coming to check if you'd like tea. You've missed supper, but there's a good spread still."

"You have tea all the way up here?" She hadn't meant to sound so astonished, but there it was. Miss Patricks always told her she needed to think before she opened her mouth, that it was important to take that small step before someone's feelings got hurt, intentional or not. But Flora? Her feelings seemed to be fine. In fact, she laughed, big and full.

"You are exactly what we need 'all the way up here,'" she said. "Whew, a real treat. Yes, you silly girl, we have tea. And biscuits. And even plates to eat from. Come downstairs, you."

Flora turned to leave, still chuckling and untying the apron strings behind her back. Mary listened to the young woman's feet on the stairs, then turning onto the main floor before checking quickly back up the hallway. There was nothing but silence now. She patted down her unruly dark curls and headed for the stairs. Perhaps she had imagined the crying after all.

# 3

# The World Outside

The dining room was bigger than the one in her Toronto house, with high ceilings and a massive table that looked like it had been carved from an entire oak tree. No less than twelve silk cushioned chairs were positioned around it, each one tucked neatly at an equal distance from the other. On the back wall was a large window with thick glass that warped the view.

That's where Mary went first, past the chairs and the trays of sweets and sandwiches laid out, to the window to look outside. Once her eyes adjusted to the waning sunlight and the world came into focus, Mary caught her breath.

The trees were close together and lush, so tight they braided their branches together like little girls holding hands. The ground was carpeted with wildflowers. There were two large greenhouses in the clearing behind the house, filled with shelves and pots and gardening tools. Beyond them were brick walls built in a pattern that couldn't be determined from any view but above. And in the very back, where the shadows began and the flowers ended, was the forest. And beyond that, the sound of water, constant and huge.

Mary had always lived in the city, so any expanse of greenery had been strictly manicured, cut neat and squared away. But this? This was . . .

"Wild," she finished her thought in a whisper.

"That's the truth of it," Flora answered from the doorway, holding a pot of tea. "And still, not so wild. I've seen wilder."

"You have?" Mary was impressed.

"I have. My Père took us on trips up the Bay. He has the sturdiest canoe and the surest paddles." She placed the pot on a place mat and walked over to join the girl at the window. "There are thousands of islands out in the water 'round here."

"Surely not *thousands*." Mary couldn't believe it, though she really wanted to. "How can that be?"

"Oh, it's true." Flora looked at her earnestly. "I've seen only about a hundred. But my Père, he's seen them all."

"Your . . . pear?" Mary asked.

"No, my Père," Flora corrected. "My grandfather."

"Your Père, does he take other people out in his canoe?" She could practically feel the wind on her cheeks, hear the sound of the oars slicing the water.

"My Père has passed on, now," Flora said quietly. "And his canoe has been in the shed house ever since."

"Oh." Mary knew she should say something. Anything. "That's too bad. I would have liked to go out with someone civilized."

Flora's silence told her she'd chosen the wrong words. Both girls turned back to the window.

"So, what do you mean, it's not so wild?" Mary continued, eager to move on. "Is the town big?"

"Oh, it's pretty small. Just half-breeds, some French farmers out the other way, soldiers and the lumber workers. It's just the land—it's not as empty as you might think. There are people all through the bush." Flora smiled a little.

"But they're . . . behaved?"

"On Sundays we are." Flora laughed, swatting at Mary playfully. "Then we go to the church with everyone else. Go now. Go and eat."

Mary picked a chair and settled in. Flora poured her tea and put a small plate in front of her so she could choose what she wanted to eat, chatting away the whole time about the weather, the mountainous snow in late winter and the thick streams of bugs in early summer. She had such a way about her stories, such a joy in her voice that when she left to return to the kitchen, Mary found herself missing the company. This was a new feeling. She ate quickly and went off in search of the kitchen.

The kitchen was large, bigger than the one in Toronto had been, though Mary couldn't be sure. She had rarely gone in there and had no real memories of it other than the smell of cleaner and a row of aprons hung along the wall for catering staff. This kitchen was all wood and tile, and smelled of fried onions and stewed meat. There was a bag of flour on the floor, and on a tall stool perched an old lady with a red kerchief tied around her head. Flora stood at a deep sink washing silver cutlery.

"I want to go for a walk now," Mary said in her best assertive voice, like the one her mother had used on the staff.

"Around here, we say please and merci," Flora chided.

Mary started to laugh—no servant had ever talked back to her, so surely this was a joke. But at the first giggle, Flora's frown deepened so that lines appeared between her eyes.

"I'm busy. And Philomene here? She doesn't like walking so much these days." Flora looked away, her mouth tight.

Philomene said nothing, just shook her head, indicating the younger woman was telling the truth.

Mary didn't know how to respond. "Well then, I shall . . . I shall go on my own."

"That's fine," Flora answered, her back still turned. "Just stick to the cleared grounds, you. I don't need to have to send Jean to find you in the woods. They get *wild* around here."

Philomene chuckled, mumbling words Mary could only

assume were French. Clearly, Flora had come back to the kitchen and told the woman what she had said.

Mary hadn't expected to be talked about, and she certainly didn't like being called on her bluff. Truthfully, she was nervous about going outside in this new place. There was bound to be all sorts of animals around here, not like the city. And even there, one could find possums or large field rats running about. Out here? She imagined lions, even though she knew lions were not native to these lands. There was just something feral and dangerous about this place that made her think of sharp teeth and yellow eyes.

"Well, I can't." She huffed, angry at having to still talk to these women. "I have no one to dress me."

"Dress you?" Flora spun around. "A big girl like you? My mother was on her own at your age. I'm sure you can put on some boots, you. And there's an old mackinaw on the coat rack you can throw on."

"A mack-in-what?"

"A mackinaw." Flora exchanged a look with the old woman, as if to say, *Does this girl know nothing?* "A wool coat. The wind's picked up. Not yet full spring."

"Argh!" Mary literally stomped her foot, which led the women to exchange another glance and then break out in a peal of laughter.

"I will not be laughed at!" Mary shouted back, stomping her foot again.

"Then you best be on your way." Flora cackled. "Because if you keep step-dancing in this kitchen, chére, we're gonna keep laughing."

Mary stormed away. She would have to speak with her uncle about their behavior. But for now, she *would* go out by herself. It was clear she would have to start doing a lot of things on her own. Incredibly, she even started to miss Miss Patricks a little.

She found galoshes in a wardrobe room by the front entrance, but they wouldn't fit over her neat black boots, and there was no way she was going to slip strange boots over her fine stockings. "You can handle a little mud, I'm sure," she said to her boots. Apparently, she was now talking aloud not only to herself, but to inanimate objects.

She found what could only be the coat Flora had suggested. It was red wool and heavy to lift and fit with just a little room left in the shoulders. Her mother would have frozen into a block of ice before she wore such a thing, but Mary liked the weight of it on her body. She felt as if she suddenly was not so alone. Which then reminded her that she was in fact very much alone.

She sat down on the boot bench, the movement like a sigh that kicked all the breath out of her chest. She felt small. She felt insubstantial. She felt like she was going to cry, which she hadn't done since she cracked her tooth last year.

"My parents are gone," she whispered—maybe to her

boots, or to the coats that hung around her like fine tailored ghosts, or to herself. "I am alone."

She felt it then, the wide emptiness of that fact, and she sniffed. That one lonesome sound, that small comma in the sentence of her day, that was what broke the dam. She sobbed into the scratchy wool of the heavy jacket where its sleeves fell over her palms.

That's where Flora found her, then guided her back to her room to weep into her pillow, which was much softer.

---

"We are going on a picnic tomorrow," Flora said, brushing Mary's hair while the girl sat at the little vanity in her room. Her face was red and puffy, her eyes still leaking from the small slits they had become. She'd spent the afternoon crying. Weeping in front of the servants was just embarrassing, but this was nice, getting her hair brushed by Flora while she chatted on about the area.

"You'll have to dress warm. Weather is unpredictable up here, about now. Even so, the trees are starting to unroll all those leaves, and soon the flowers will be back. Then we can go medicine picking with my mother."

It seemed odd to Mary that Flora should have a life outside of her job at the manor. As soon as she thought it, even she knew that was a ridiculous thing to think. She remembered

Brandy McCarthy—the real Brandy McCarthy and not the one that made her stomach feel funny in her dream. *The snobbiest snot ever to live.*

Feeling fragile and lulled by the rhythmic slide and pull of the brush, Mary wanted nothing more than to imagine things outside her own life. "Tell me about her? Your mom . . . please."

Flora smiled at Mary in the mirror. "My mother, she is a tiny woman, like most women in the community. Her own Mère and Père, they came over from Drummond Island after the war, when they pushed the half-breeds to leave. They settled with the others in Penetanguishene and built a house the way they used to back home, close together with enough room between for a sugar bush."

The war? Mary ran through dates and events from her history tutor's lessons. Must be the War of 1812. She didn't know Native people had been in that war. It made sense, but none of the books mentioned them.

"My mother, she has seven of us. I am the oldest, then Benjamin, then Sophie, Louis, Rose, Marie, and finally little Frederic who has just turned one. There is sixteen years between Fred and I, so he's like my own sweet baby."

That meant Flora was seventeen. How was she just two years older than Mary? She seemed so mature, so capable. A new wave of embarrassment spread over Mary's skin. This girl, not much older than her, had both chastised her and comforted her today.

"Oh, you would love Sophie. She's your age exactly and such a bright soul. She knows these lands better than almost anyone. 'Course she spent all her days with our Père before he passed on. That's where the real learning always comes from, those old ones." Flora smiled. "She can fish and hunt and knows all the plants, too. And she's not shy about doing what they call women's work or men's jobs at the same. She doesn't care what those other ones say at all."

This both shocked and appealed to Mary. A boy who didn't care seemed like a magical being. All the boys she had ever met did nothing but care how others' thought of them, always competing, always puffing out their chests. But a *girl* who didn't care? Who wasn't worried about appearances or what people might say, things that could affect marriage prospects or start rumors?

A girl like that seemed impossible.

"Does Sophie ever come to the manor?" Mary asked.

"Sometimes, when Maman can spare her. And when she's not out on a hunt." Flora sighed. "Oh, I miss that good food from home. I only get there once a week, on Sundays. But when I do go home, mon dieu, the *food*. On Sundays you'd never guess we are anything but rich, even in our little cabin."

"I want to know all about it," Mary said. "Tell me everything."

Flora laughed, putting the brush down on the vanity counter. "Why don't you just come with me one Sunday?"

"Me? Come to your house?" Mary was shocked. Again, Brandy's voice was in her head. *And the girl? She was awful.*

"Of course." Flora turned down the quilts on Mary's bed, fluffed her pillows, and then made for the door. "There's a whole world outside. You don't have to be like—" She paused, stumbling a bit. "Like Mr. Craven and just stay indoors. There is so much to see. And we'll start tomorrow."

Then she bid her bonsoir and closed the door behind her, leaving Mary sitting in front of the mirror. Suddenly she was uncomfortable, as if Flora had taken all the air in the room with her. She didn't want to see her reflection, all pathetic and swollen, so she stood and went to the window instead.

It was dark now, and the land behind the house had disappeared in the shadows, layered like tulle, deep blue to softest black. But she could hear the water—it was always close by, like a constant whisper. She wondered just what would be waiting for her out there in the world. Then she lay down in her bed and waited for sleep.

Tomorrow she would ask Flora for paper and ink and if there were any books lying around the house. But for tonight, she tried to imagine herself in a tree swing with a friend, one whose eyelashes curled on her cheek and whose hand she was aching to touch.

# 4

# A Secret in the Woods

THE NEXT DAY, IT WAS SUNNY AND WARM, THE KIND OF DAY THAT feels like a reprieve, like a gift. Mary wasn't used to getting gifts, so she grabbed an umbrella, wore her big winter coat, and packed an extra sweater and gloves for when early May gave up the ruse and things returned to normal.

Flora chuckled. "Holy, you're a real optimist, aren't you? It's not gonna snow now. That's passed us."

"Could rain, still." Mary pursed her lips. "And I don't like to get wet."

"You need to loosen up, you. A little rain never hurt nobody. You're not made of sugar," Flora said. But seeing Mary start to put back her umbrella, she relented. "I'm only teasing. Me and my siblings, we do it all the time to each other. Bring your umbrella if it makes you feel better. Don't bother with what I say."

Mary felt a small spark of joy. Flora was treating her like her brothers and sisters? Maybe she would go to her cabin with her. Maybe there would be something—she wasn't sure what, but *something*—there for her. She leaned her umbrella against the wall. She wouldn't need it.

Outside they caught up to Jean, who was heading down to the Bay with a fishing pole slung over his shoulder.

"You heading our way, then?" Flora called cheerfully.

The older man paused, turned back to watch them walk across the uneven grass, and kept going without a word. The three of them went on together in silence, past the greenhouses and into the trees.

They passed two blocked-off areas made of round stones cobbled together into seven-foot walls. "What are these?" Mary asked.

"Those are Mr. Craven's gardens. He wanted them to be like back in England. Had to use rocks, like back home, he said. Even though the man made his fortune in the lumberyards here. No, no wood for the gardens. They had to be English or not at all." Flora clucked her tongue. "Boy, that took some doing."

"They're lovely," Mary said. She liked the way brown

tendrils snaked up the sides. Soon they would be green and bursting with leaves. She loved vines. The library by her house in Toronto had been covered in vines. In the summer, you could barely see out the windows, and the light came in filtered green so that the whole room seemed to be outside, but without the wet and dirt. "Can I go in?"

Jean and Flora exchanged a quick look, but not so quick that Mary didn't notice. "Yes, of course," Flora said. "In a bit, we'll go in. There's not much to see right now. Jean will have to start preparing them soon enough. You can help."

"Help?" Mary was confused. She wanted to enjoy the gardens, not *work* in them. What was wrong with her uncle's staff? Did they not know that she was a guest? Still, she didn't say another word. The teasing she'd gotten from Flora in the mudroom was still blooming warm inside her chest, and she didn't want to make the older girl cross.

Flora ignored the indignant tone in Mary's response. "Sure. Sophie always comes around to help Jean in the gardens. It'll be fun. There's birds nested in there and all kinds of creepy-crawly things for her to study."

"That does not sound like fun," Mary replied. But, desperate to meet Sophie, the girl who braved the forests and lake by herself, she added, "But maybe. It could be . . . All right, I'll help."

Jean did not look impressed. How was he not impressed? Miss Patricks would have died of a heart attack if Mary had agreed to wash one dish. Well, there was no accounting for manners, she supposed. Maybe she would rub off on them. She would be a good influence.

Within the trees, it was colder. The sun was blocked out by the tall trunks and massive branches. There were enough evergreens to make the empty birch and sleeping oaks seem less skeletal. The ground was mushy, not having dried out in this darkness, and she could smell the richness of thawing soil. Every now and then, the path would veer close to another rock wall.

"How many are there?" Mary asked.

Flora stopped her constant chatter to Jean, who had still not said a word to answer her. "What's that?"

"Gardens. How many are there?"

"Uh, six," Flora answered. "Six gardens you can go into, and you will when you start lendin' your hands to it."

They carried on, Mary cautiously stepping over unearthed roots and around thick brush. She counted the gardens as they went. Indeed there were six squared areas, each with an arched wooden door set into a rock wall. Over the snap of twigs and the shuffle of dried leaves was the static sound of movement. It grew louder as they walked on. Even so, she was not prepared for the sudden change from woods to beach.

It was like walking into a well-lit room, like the great room where Mother held her parties, all chandeliers and linen-draped tables. Only this was a hundredfold. The sun reflected off the dark blue water and the white sand at different volumes, each glaring and full.

Here in front of the waters of the Georgian Bay, her feet planted in the still-firm sand after winter's freeze, Mary felt smaller than she ever had even in the bustle of the city. She moved closer to Flora, who put an arm around the girl's shoulders.

"She's tres beaux, eh?" Flora sighed, like she was in love. "Look out there, you see those shadows out there? Those are some of the bigger islands. And look at the trees out here. Those are our trees."

Mary tried to focus on these things and not on the enormity of the scene. She did see the shadowy island. And the trees were different than any she had ever seen before. They looked as if they were being pulled out to the water, leaning and holding their wooden arms out in offering. They looked as if they were in a wild windstorm even though the day was still and calm.

"Okay then." Flora took her arm away and clapped her hands neatly. "Let's set up."

They spent an hour or so there, eating sandwiches with the crusts still on. (Mary left those on her napkin so Flora would know better next time, and then watched with disgust when instead Jean picked them up and ate them himself.) Flora talked about fishing—where to drop a line and how to use a net, things that Mary found both boring and unladylike.

They finished a thermos of juice and then went to the shoreline to pick up interesting rocks and shells. The sound of the water lapping at their feet and the weight of the juice in her stomach made Mary have to use the bathroom.

"Where are the facilities?" she asked Flora, who was washing flat stones in the tide before tossing them out to skip on the glittery lake.

"Facilities?" Flora scrunched up her nose, then tossed a rock, skipping it three times. She lifted her arms in victory then turned back. "Oh, facilities. Well, in summer, this lake would be your facilities."

"Disgusting," Mary scoffed. "Never."

"Oh, you'd be surprised how hard it is to hold when you're waist-deep in the lake. But the water is cold yet, will be for another six weeks. For now"—she pointed to the trees—"this way, my lady."

Mary crossed her arms over her chest. She was about to stomp her foot when she remembered being laughed at in the kitchen for just that very thing. "I will not do my business in the trees."

"Well." Flora crossed her arms the same way. "How badly do you have to go?"

Mary looked about sheepishly. "Fine! But I need a napkin. And I need privacy." She was angry and embarrassed, but she really couldn't hold it.

She tromped back into the woods and left the worn path, wandering in to where the evergreens provided more cover. When she was done, she left the napkin on the ground and buried it, kicking dirt over the fabric with the toe of her shoe. She was annoyed. Why would they bring her to a place with no civilized way to pee? *How humiliating.* She adjusted her skirts and straightened her tights then started to walk back to the beach.

Except at some point, she had gotten turned around. Everything looked the same out here. She turned in a circle and was about to call out when she thought of Sophie. Sophie wouldn't call for help. So instead she listened. She could hear Flora laughing. She just needed to follow the sound. But then something different caught her attention, and she walked away from the reassuring laughter.

A wall. Stacked rocks and smoothed corners—another garden! But on this one, there were so many vines it looked as if there had been a green explosion inside, and the smoke came out in tendrils, draping over the outer walls. There was no path leading to this garden, and the door, when she found it, was almost completely hidden by old greenery. She walked the entire perimeter twice, running her hands along the stone where it was visible and examining the vines. Many were covered in sharp spikes. She knew this plant. She remembered their bright beauty and their prickly stems well.

"Roses," she said brightly. What were distinguished roses doing out here in the wilds?

"Mary!" Flora was calling her. "Mary, are you all right?"

"Yes," she called back. "I'm fine. Over here!"

There was some noise of crunching branches and underbrush, and then Flora appeared with Jean, who was carrying the basket.

"We packed up and you still weren't back. What ha . . ." Seeing where Mary was standing, her voice trailed off.

"I thought you said there were only six gardens? This would make seven." Mary tried the door, but it wouldn't budge. "I want to see this one. It looks different."

"I said there were six you could go into. This one you can't."

Her tone was a bit clipped, Mary noticed. But instead of backing off, she pushed. "I want to go into this one, and since it is on my uncle's property and you work for my uncle, then you need to do as I say."

"Oh, so I have to listen now, is it?" Flora tried to be firm, but there was something else in her voice, something like fear. "Well, let me tell you this, Mademoiselle de Toronto. It was your uncle himself that locked that up. Gave orders that it should never be opened again. It's stood locked for fourteen years now, since the first Mrs. Craven died, and I don't think a wee girl like you is going to change his mind."

Without waiting for an answer, Flora started off, heading back to the main path.

Mary sighed. There was something about this garden. She wanted to see what was inside more than anything else. She couldn't explain it, but it was like there was something in there that was meant for her.

"Tha key."

She startled. Did Jean just speak? She had started to think that he couldn't. "What's that?"

"Tha key is 'ere somewhere. He hid it. You need that." He looked as surprised at the sound of his own words as Mary was. "Then you go in."

He turned and walked away. Alone now in a part of the woods she had already gotten lost in once, in front of a mysterious locked door, Mary picked up her feet and ran after him.

A secret garden in the woods! She felt more awake than she could ever remember feeling before.

---

Before they left the woods, Flora had regained composure, working to leave the secret garden behind them with all the conversations that might come from its discovery. Mary, however, could think of nothing else. But she knew enough to keep her mouth shut about it.

She walked briskly back to the yard, taking the lead when the trees gave way to field. The house looked dark and imposing from here. She thought about the museum and even some of the photos her father had kept in his office of important buildings back in Britain.

And then she stopped, because from the round window in the very top and center of the house was a person looking down at her.

"Who is that?"

Flora caught up to where Mary was standing. "Who's what?"

Mary pointed at the window, and the figure moved, jumping out of sight. "Up there. Someone in a white dress."

"I didn't see anyone," Flora answered. But something in her voice made Mary think she had indeed seen something.

"Like a child, or a small woman, maybe." Mary squinted, using her hand as a visor over her eyes.

"Come on now." Flora hooked her arm through the younger girl's. "Probably just the sun reflecting off the glass."

"No, I saw them!" Mary refused to be pulled forward, pushing all her weight into her feet. "They were right there, wearing a white shift!"

Jean walked slowly past and spoke again, as if the cork had been pulled and he was now free to drop words. His voice was low and grumbly. "Maybe what she's saying, chére, is that she can't talk about whatcha seen."

Flora bit her lip. Mary saw the stress on her face and relented, allowing herself to be guided up the rest of the yard and back into the cool, dark house.

---

After she had been in bed for some time and the sounds from the rest of the house had settled, Mary pulled off her quilts, swung her legs to the side of the bed, and stood. She crept to the door and put her ear against it, listening for voices or the clatter of pans in the kitchen. Nothing. She knew Flora and Philomene slept in a small bedroom on the main floor and that the men went to their own homes nearby, so she had the whole second floor to herself.

Well, her and whoever that person was in the window this afternoon. And she was about to find out.

Mary carefully lit a small oil lamp by her bed—electricity was limited to the main rooms. She stepped into her soft slippers and pulled on a robe. Then, the lamp in one hand, she opened her door.

The hallway was eerie in the dark, only lit by a small circle of lamplight like a small moon. The shadows gathered and arched and made it seem overly huge and intimately cramped at the same time. Mary listened again—there was some ticking of old wood and the wind rattling a loose window downstairs, but nothing else.

"Come on, why aren't you crying tonight?" Mary whispered. She wasn't sure which way to turn. Being able to follow a noise would have been a big help. She sighed, picked left, and started down the hall.

Every ten feet or so, there was a door. The first one she tried opened up into a room containing a massive four-poster bed with a dust sheet thrown over the bedding. There were other draped shapes in the room like angular ghosts—furniture, she guessed. The window had the same view as the one from her room—the backyard, the two greenhouses, garden walls, and the perimeter of trees. She tiptoed back out and closed the door as quietly as she could.

The next room was a dressing room, with long wooden wardrobes built into the walls on three sides. When she opened one, it was full of meticulously pressed jackets. The next had tailored slacks, and a third held rows of perfectly shined men's shoes. There was a full-length mirror and a smaller cabinet with the tools necessary to keep the inventory starched and shining—cans of polish, darkened rags, a heavy iron. In the corner was a wingback chair. The whole room smelled of old pipe smoke. This must be where Uncle Craven dressed. She wondered where he even went in such fine clothes. Surely there was nothing important around here to do, no meetings, no social events.

The next room was an office. This was the most boring of the rooms. Her father had one just like it back in Toronto—

used to have one just like it, she reminded herself. Every office was exactly the same to Mary—an overbearing desk, leather-bound books, a pen in a stand, a blotter on the surface.

Mary set the lamp down on the desk and walked around to the front. She pulled the chair back, and it screeched against the floorboards. She drew in a sharp breath and eyed the door, waiting. After a moment when no one came, she carefully lifted the chair as best she could and pulled it again. Then she tried the top drawer.

Locked. "Dammit."

She went to the side and tried each one there—all locked. On the right side, she grabbed the top drawer and it opened. She had been expecting it to be locked like the rest, so she almost pulled it straight from the desk and onto the floor, but she managed to stop it with her hip. Inside she found what she wanted: a bottle of ink, an old pen with a crusty nib—not a worry, she could clean that right up—and a stack of creamy paper.

She took the bottle, pen, and only four pages—she didn't want to get in trouble for taking more than she needed. She shoved her treasures in the pockets of her dressing gown and made her way back to the door, the lamp held aloft.

She almost turned and went back to her room. She had paper and ink for her lists and plans, and that was good enough. But then she heard it—a thin cry, and it was coming from farther down the hall.

"There you are . . ." Mary turned toward the sound and followed it. She put her ear up against a few doors, but there was nothing. Finally, after taking a left turn at the end of the hall—this house really was gigantic—she came upon a narrow door. She had to stand on a small step to reach the handle. It wasn't until she had the knob in her hand that she realized she was shaking.

What if it was a ghost? Maybe it was the first Mrs. Craven haunting her home. What if it was an animal, injured and ready to attack? Mother always said the best thing you can do for an injured animal is to bash it in the head. Would she be able to do that? And even so, could she do it before she was clawed to death? There was that image of a lion again, a great maned man-eater isolated on the Georgian Bay and trapped in a distant room.

"No, this is a person," she said out loud to herself. "I saw you."

She turned the handle quickly before she could change her mind. On the other side was a steep staircase leading up.

Mary took a deep breath and held it, then tiptoed up the creaky, old steps. She couldn't see what was up at the top—it was too dark still. She paused to look back once. The open door was a lighter shade of black against the total darkness of the stairwell.

She considered going back. She didn't want to make Flora angry. Right now, the friendly young housekeeper was the only person in the whole world she could talk to. Then there came a series of small sniffs from somewhere above.

*That's no lion*, she thought. She pushed all the breath out of her body and took the last steps with squared shoulders. *I am not afraid of a ghost, certainly not one who is so whiny.*

At the top of the stairs, Mary came to a door. She put her hand on the knob and turned it . . . and it moved, unlocked.

She took a moment, pursing her lips, then pushed the door open.

She was ready to come face-to-face with the ghost in the attic.

# 5

# Olive's Haunting

The room was enormous; it must have run the entire length of one of the wings, bigger than Mary's quarters by ten. The space looked like a small church—high ceiling, a stained glass window on one end and the round window she'd seen from the yard on the other. There were candles lit here and there flickering in the breeze seeping in through the cracks in the windowsill. The corners stayed in the shadows, and mismatched pieces of heavy furniture were scattered about, as if this was the place they were brought to once they were outdated or had outlived their usefulness.

There were four long tables placed against the wall on either side of a dark fireplace mantle that had been stripped free of the hearth. Each one was covered with books and candles of varying height. A pale green velvet wing chair perched on a round fiber rug under the round window and across from it lay a pile of faded velvet pillows in different hues that must have once been vibrant. A few feet from that stood a wooden rocking horse.

The last item left Mary confused. What was a child's toy doing up here? There were no children in this house. As far as she knew, there never had been. All the fear from the stairwell had dissolved into curiosity, and that was much stronger than any fear she might have had. There was a mystery here, and she would have none of it.

What exactly was this place? It seemed a bit grimy, a bit like a storage room, except there were details that could not be explained. For example, hanging in the middle of the room from the rafters was a huge chandelier, finer than any she had had back home. It was unlit, but the flickering of the candles below caught the crystals and threw small shards of light. The floor, she soon realized, was covered in overlapping rugs in all styles—Turkish runners and Persian squares, even rounded mats made of woven straw.

Mary stepped into the room and turned, holding up the lantern to see along the walls. More shelves and more books! Oh, what a library! Then there were cabinets, wardrobes, and a low shelf filled with a neat line of tiny shoes, highly polished and brand-new looking.

There came a sniff from the shadows.

Mary spun, lifting her lantern. Against the far wall, under the stained glass of bright purple flowers and long green leaves, was a bed completely cloaked in heavy damask drapery.

She cleared her throat and took a step. "Hello? Is someone there?"

There was no reply.

"You know it's rude not to answer," Mary said, approaching the bed. "It's insolent." She recycled words her own mother had said to her. "And not polite."

"I'm pretty sure coming into someone's bedroom uninvited is also not polite."

The voice belonged to a girl, and it was definitely coming from the bed. Mary was no longer afraid. She stood at the foot and yanked back one of the drapes. In the midst of layers of blankets and piles of pillows was a girl around her own age.

"Who are you?" Mary asked. There was something strangely familiar about her . . .

The girl replied with a series of questions. "Who are *you*? How are you here? Am I dreaming?"

Mary, deciding this thin creature was no threat, placed her lantern on the floor and set about pulling the drapes back on their hooks so that the entire bed was exposed to the candlelight.

"I am Mary Craven. Mr. Craven is my uncle, and I have come to stay with him. I just arrived from Toronto." She said the last part with a tilted chin, very proud of herself for being from such an important place. "I am the master's niece, and I demand to know who you are."

"You must be very happy to have come here, then. Away from all those people and smoke."

"What an odd thing to say!" Obviously this girl knew nothing. "Toronto is an amazing city, modern and very proper with so many cultured people. This place is somewhere to run *from*, and Toronto is a place to run *to*."

The girl moved her lips funny, like she was biting the inside of her cheek. "Hmm. You must have had a hundred friends then. Must have been sad to leave them all."

For a moment Mary thought she was being made fun of, but there was no malice in the girl's eyes. "Yes. I . . . I did have many friends. So many. And it was sad. They threw me a big bon voyage party. There was so much weeping." She sat on the edge of the mattress. "But anyway, who are you and why are you up here?"

"I'm Olive Craven. And since Mr. Craven is your uncle and he is also my father, then I suppose that makes us cousins."

The portrait, downstairs in the front hall—that's why she looked so familiar. She looked like the painting of the first Mrs. Craven, her deceased aunt. This girl was thinner, to be sure, and pale, but her eyes were unmistakable.

"Hattie was your mother?"

"You knew her?" The girl hoisted herself up and leaned

forward. "How is that possible? She died when I was a baby, and you don't look much older than me."

"There's a painting of her downstairs. And I didn't know any of you existed until two days ago."

Olive sighed. "Not many people know I exist. Rebecca says it's better that way. Says visitors would only make me sicker, so I have to stay up here."

"Who's Rebecca?"

Olive blushed. "My stepmother. Sorry, you must think I am so rude. I am to call her Mother, but I often forget."

Mary harrumphed. "If I had a stepmother who told me to stay in the attic, I would call her by her first name, too. If not worse." She felt a kinship that made her immediately protective of Olive. Mary had never had someone be so open with her right off the bat. She had never had a relative who claimed her without hesitation, and it opened up something new inside her.

Both girls paused for a moment, then broke out laughing.

"I am already glad you're here, Mary." Olive settled back on her pillows gingerly, as if she were made of glass.

"What kind of sick are you, anyway?" Mary knew it was rude to ask such a personal and forward question, but this girl was her cousin, after all. She had never had a cousin before, but she assumed that meant they were to be open books with each other.

"Oh, they don't know. The doctor says it's a nervous condition, but Rebecca says it's bound to be something much worse. I don't have any energy, and it hurts to move about."

"All the time?"

Olive considered for a moment. "No, not all the time. Mostly after I take my medicine." She pointed to a brown bottle and large spoon laid out on the side table.

"Well, that's easy, then," Mary retorted. "Don't take your medicine."

"Oh, I wish it was that simple," Olive said. "Rebecca says if I don't take it, I'll get so sick that I'll have to be brought to the sanitorium. Everyone knows that's a place you don't usually come back from."

"I don't know," Mary pressed. "I think that if something makes you feel bad, you avoid it."

Olive laughed. "That's the opposite of what Flora says. She says if something makes you feel bad, then you have to push through and get to the other side of it."

"How are you going to get to the other side of anything if you're too sick to move?" Mary countered.

This stumped Olive and she went quiet.

"Anyway, maybe you're just taking too much." Mary's voice was a bit pinched, which was what happened when she started getting upset. "So Flora knows you're up here?"

Olive nodded.

"Oh." Mary tried to sound casual, but in truth she was angry. Flora knew there was another girl—her own flesh and blood—just upstairs, and never said a word?

"Flora isn't allowed to talk about me," Olive said, easily reading her cousin's face. "She told me you were coming, but only when Rebecca had already left. And she told me not to say a word. I'm not supposed to be around anyone."

Mary straightened her back and pulled her chin in toward her chest. "You're not contagious, are you?"

"No." Olive sighed again. "But I may as well be. No one wants to be around me. I can't do normal things without breaking out into bumps."

"Bumps like measles?"

"Bumps like hives. Flora calls them nerve bumps." Olive pulled up the billowy sleeves of her nightgown to her elbows and twisted her arms in the soft lamplight. "Nothing now. Maybe you don't bring out my nerves."

For the first time, she smiled and Mary caught her breath. She was so pretty when she smiled, even more like the painting of her mother in the foyer. That she was a different version of herself—a happier, lighter version—around Mary made her feel proud, made her feel even more ferociously protective. She wasn't about to let herself be separated from the first person to welcome her without hesitation.

"Well then," Mary said. "That settles it. I am good for you, and also I am lonely. I'd bet you are, too. So I shall come and visit you every day. And no one can stop me!" She raised her index finger with this, as if making a solemn proclamation.

"I'd bet someone could, but I hope they don't," Olive said, giggling a bit. It was a light sound, like a shell cracking.

They spent another hour chatting, catching up on the entirety of their small lives, sharing everything that could even remotely be interesting or necessary in the work of building a lifelong friendship in the course of one hurried night. They spoke of dead mothers and flowers they liked, the strained way fathers spoke and the need for absolute quiet when trying to pull up a memory. They both loved bees but hated wasps, and both girls preferred strawberry jam to any other flavor.

When Olive started to yawn, Mary stood up from the bed, starting to feel sleepy herself.

"I am off to bed and then tomorrow, I will come back."

"Wait!" Olive cried as Mary turned to go. "Don't tell Flora you saw me!"

"Why not? Flora is our servant," Mary scoffed.

"Oh dear, you have a lot to learn about how this place runs. Flora is more than a servant. And I don't want to get her in trouble. If my stepmother finds out you were up here, she'll think Flora told, and then she'll send her away. I don't know what I'd do then." Olive bit her lip and scratched at her bare forearm. Mary saw the beginnings of a red swell on her skin. Hives.

"Okay, okay, don't worry. I will come back every night at

this time, and it will be our secret," Mary conceded. Then added, "For now."

Mary closed the door softly behind her and carefully made her way down the stairs. She hurried on tiptoes all the way back to her room, hardly breathing until her own bedroom door was carefully closed and locked. Then she leaned against it and let all the air in her body out.

There was an odd flutter in her chest, and she placed her hand over it. Her heart beat fast and heavy with excitement. She'd had an adventure in a spooky old house in a strange place, and for her bravery she got what she knew would be a real friend. Better than that, even—she got family.

She carried her lamp to the small desk and, pulling her paper and ink out of her pocket, dipped her pen and began to write. Across the top of a fresh sheet, she carefully spelled out the title of her latest list:

*Ways to Get Olive Craven (Aged 14 Years) Out of the Attic*

# 6

# Every Friendship Needs a Stage

The next morning, Mary was up and out of the house before Flora could serve tea. She had barely slept, and adrenaline made it difficult to be idle. She went out into the backyard and counted the steps from the door to a spot on the grass where she was certain Olive could see her if she looked down. She found a round, smooth stone and placed it there. This would be where she would stand to communicate with her during the day, until everyone was asleep and she could sneak up to the attic for a visit. She stood there, her hand over her eyes once the sun came up, willing Olive to the window.

"What has caught your mind?"

Mary jumped. She hadn't seen Flora come out the back door. The girl stood beside her now, trying to see what it was that Mary was staring at.

"Ah, a . . . a bird, a big one. I think it must be an eagle," Mary stammered. "It was on the roof for a while. Must have taken off when you came out."

Flora laughed. "Most likely a vulture. People, they're confused about that all the time, as if they look even a bit alike. But maybe an eagle. Who knows?"

They stood there for a moment, Mary keeping up the charade by scanning the sky in all directions.

"Well, let's go in for breakfast, then. Philomene didn't believe me when I said you were already up and out." Flora put her hand on Mary's back and guided her inside.

Mary had never had a secret this big—literally a girl-size secret. As a matter of fact, other than her lists and the small paragraphs she wrote up and then folded into tiny shapes and threw in the fireplace, she had never had a secret at all. She found herself humming her way through her eggs and toast. Flora watched her curiously from the other side of the table.

"I like that we eat together," Mary said, offhanded.

"Oh, don't get used to all this." Flora chuckled. "When the grown-ups are home, me? I eat in the kitchen."

"Then I shall eat in the kitchen, too," Mary declared, lifting her fork like a gavel and tapping it on the edge of her plate for emphasis.

"Oh you will, now?"

"Yes, I will." Mary nodded her head once, solemnly. "Why would I want to eat with strangers?"

"Because they are your people?" Flora suggested. "Monsieur Craven is your own uncle."

"I don't know him. We have never met." Mary meant it to be casual, but once she said it, the statement brought questions along with it. "Why do you suppose that is?"

"How am I to know?" Flora scoffed. "Some people forget that they come from somewhere, that they belong to people and a place. That makes it easier, I think."

"Easier for what?"

"To act for only yourself." Flora pushed her chair back and stood, starting to clean the plates. "Me? I may be carrying weight—my brothers, my sisters, my own mother. And that means I act from there, from under that weight. But also, it means I can never just blow away, me. I am held steady. It's a good burden. The best one."

Mary placed her fork on the table. She wasn't hungry anymore. "Flora? Do you think that's what's wrong with me?"

The older girl furrowed her brow. "What can you mean?"

"Why I'm so angry. Why I feel all frustrated and could kick things. Do you think I am just . . . blowing around?" Her voice was low. She felt a kind of shame just then.

"You?" Flora put the dirty plates down in a clatter. "You are too young to be thinking those things. And now you have me. I'm weight enough when I want to be, and I want to be." She grabbed up the girl in a quick hug, pushing her tight against her chest so that Mary could smell smoke and mint. Then she released her quickly, knowing the strange girl who had been left in her care was not one for sentiment.

"Now, you go find yourself some adventure, you."

Mary sat quietly at the empty table for a moment, alone. To an outsider watching, she resembled a serious child deep in thought, perhaps a moment of remorse or contemplation. But really, it was the picture of a strange girl who had never before been held out of affection; a child who had just for the first time felt the beginning stirrings of belonging.

She sat there with her eyes closed and tried to memorize every detail of the way she felt. Then she skipped out into the backyard to search for early May flowers. She wanted to bring something from the outside to her cousin's attic.

---

"They go to bed pretty early here. But back in Toronto, my parents were up all hours. Mostly they went out to other people's houses for dinners or cards or cocktails. But once in a while the people came to our place."

"Wow." Olive was sitting up in bed, a little more color in her cheeks than last night. "That sounds exciting. We've never had a party here."

"When you're better, we'll throw a party," Mary said, fussing with the bed curtains. She was trying to draw them back and tie them up so Olive had a view of the entire room. "We will order food and floral arrangements and Jean will wear one of those little bowties and walk around with a silver tray serving champagne with strawberry slices." She minced about, hunching her back and scowling to imitate the big gardener holding out a tray. The girls laughed.

"I don't think you could convince him to do it. Jean is not a domestic." Olive giggled. She patted the bed beside her so her cousin would sit. "Tell me about the shore again."

Mary threw herself onto the quilt. "It's not like anything I've seen before. There's a lake in the city, a big one, too. And they've built a wooden boardwalk so you can go from one edge to the next, before the sand turns into rock. On warm weekends, there are people there, women with lace umbrellas and men with ridiculous mustaches. And they take their shoes off and walk along the edge. But here? Here it's not like that. It doesn't feel like a place to dip your toes or watch the horizon."

"What does it feel like?" Olive was leaning in.

"Here, it feels different. Big and small at the same time. No, that's not really it. It's kind of like . . ." Mary struggled to find the words. "It's like, in the city, the lake is today. And here, the lake is tomorrow and yesterday at the same time."

Olive closed her eyes and took a deep breath. "It's history and possibility."

"Yes," Mary agreed. "That's it. And the sand is so white. It's like powdered sugar."

"Sometimes, Flora sneaks me treats," Olive confided, grabbing Mary's hands. "And it's the best thing ever. Rhubarb tarts, fried dough, even one time a maple sugar lolly she made with her mother. Ugh!" She threw herself back on the mattress as if in a dead faint. "I love maple treats!"

Mary had an idea. "We need to have a baking day."

Olive moved her hand from over her eyes where she had thrown it dramatically. "A what?"

"A baking day!" Mary scrambled to her knees. "I've never had one—Mother never let me in the kitchen. That was for the cook only. But we can do it here! We can plan a day, send Flora for the ingredients and make all the sweets we want!"

Olive didn't seem to share her cousin's enthusiasm, so Mary began to bounce on her knees, then clambered to her feet and jumped on the bed. "We'll make cakes, and a pie, and—oh, a strudel! I had one once, when Father was hosting some dignitaries. I snuck right into the pantry and ripped off a big chunk for myself. We'll make the biggest strudel ever made!"

"Stop," Olive mumbled, grabbing her stomach as she was jostled about.

"I'll talk to Flora tomorrow. We can do it the day after—"

"STOP!"

Mary tried to be still mid-bounce, stumbling over her footing, falling to the mattress beside her cousin. Her skin looked green. "Olive, are you all right?"

The girl suddenly opened her eyes wide and clapped a hand over her mouth, then scrambled to lean over the edge of the bed. She managed to fumble a chamber pot from under the bed skirts before vomiting. Mary held back the girl's long dark hair.

"I'm so sorry. Oh, Olive, here, let me get you back under the covers." She carefully maneuvered the girl back against the pillows and then set about cleaning up the mess. There was a small water closet up here, something that looked as though it had been added as an afterthought. It held a small toilet and a sink with a single faucet that only carried lukewarm water, no matter how long you left it on. Mary wet a cloth and gently wiped Olive's face. She wasn't green anymore, but she remained pale.

"Are you all right? Do you need the pot again?"

Olive, her eyes closed, shook her head.

"I'm going to rinse this out," she said, gathering up the chamber pot. "I'll be right back."

In the bathroom, Mary held her breath. The mess was foul, acrid, and almost black in color. She rinsed it out quickly and brought the clean bowl back to the bed.

Olive seemed a bit better now. "Do you want me to leave you?" Mary whispered, not sure if she was making things worse, and certain she was to blame for the whole ordeal. "I am so sorry."

"About what?" Olive's voice was a bit rough.

"For talking about food and bouncing you about. I made you sick."

"Oh that?" Olive smiled weakly. "I mean, maybe, but the truth is, I throw up a lot. It's the medicine. Rebecca says that's how I know it's working, getting the disease out."

"You're still taking it, then?"

"I did, but half of what I'm supposed to," Olive finished with a sigh. "I'm going to try, like you said. Just take a little less every time, so they don't notice. Maybe I'll feel better."

Mary wrinkled her nose. "Olive, I thought you were sick in your nerves."

"I am, why?"

"Well . . ." Mary arranged the pillows around the girl's head and folded down the quilt so that she was tucked in nicely. "Last I checked, nerves aren't in your stomach."

"Where are they, then?"

Mary sat gently at the edge, having learned her lesson about jostling her cousin about. "I don't know, Olive. I'm not a doctor. Your head, maybe?"

They laughed together, more subdued than earlier. Olive looked tired and Mary knew she should leave her to rest, but she didn't want to go, not yet. "Olive?"

"Yes," she answered, her eyes closed.

"Did you know about me? I mean, did you know that I existed down in the city? Did you wonder about me, what I was doing, what I looked like?"

She opened her eyes and looked at Mary. There was such a longing in her eyes it was hard to hold her gaze, but she did. "My father, he doesn't spend much time . . . with me. He loves me, I know that. Flora says that's why he can't stay up here long. It hurts him to see me like this. And then I look so much like my mother, and he never got over her. Not even when Rebecca came along. So we don't talk much, us. I knew he had a brother and that he was an important man down in the city, but that was it."

Olive pulled her arm out from under the covers and took Mary's hand. "If I had known you existed, I would have found you. If I had to walk there on my own two feet, or rolled there in a wagon wheel, I would have found you."

"You would?"

"I would."

Mary stayed there until Olive's breathing was long and even. Then she turned off the light and crept back down the stairs to her own room.

She fell asleep right away, comforted by a new, gentle weight.

---

Every night they tried to pack in as much as possible, making up for lost time in the hours between the house falling asleep and their own exhaustion calling an end to their visits. In pajamas and messy hair, they tried folding origami, something Mary had learned from her former math tutor. They only succeeded in making the kind of cranes that couldn't possibly take flight.

"Mine looks like a fat chicken," Olive lamented. Mary laughed until she had to rush to the toilet lest she wet herself.

Then they tried their hand at dancing.

"We can't have music, so how are we going to do this?" Mary had found an old violin in a box, but half the strings were snapped.

"Even if that thing could play," Olive reminded her, "we couldn't play it. It's too loud. Maybe Philomene might sleep through, but Flora? Flora'd be up here in a flash, her."

"Maybe we can sing? But low, because I can't carry a tune anyway."

"Then we hum," Olive said.

The girls arranged themselves like a proper gentleman and a proper lady, albeit in bare feet and long shifts. Clasping hands, they hummed their way through a clumsy waltz. They ended by collapsing on the bed, giggling.

The activity that lured them into committing the most hours was needlepoint.

"Rebecca left a hoop up here once. Not on purpose, mind you. It was hers and it was terrible. I think she was supposed to be doing her initials, but it looked like a child's drawing of a spider," Olive said, pulling a wooden embroidery hoop out from under her bed. "So I took it all out."

"She didn't notice it was gone?"

"Her? She doesn't notice anything that isn't her own self." Olive pointed by tipping her chin toward a dresser in the far corner. "Top drawer there's a kit—an old kit, but it still works."

Mary opened the drawer and shifted the contents—old patterns cut from thick felt, a shoe shine set that still smelled of oil, a creepy porcelain doll with only one working eye that opened and snapped shut when you moved her. Under a canvas, half painted with the profile of a black dog, she found the embroidery things. There was no hoop, but a bundle of threads, a packet of needles, and a meter of cream-colored fabric wrapped around the rest.

"Sometimes she plays at her role, you know?"

"What's that?" Mary struggled to close the drawer quietly. The wood was old and warped and squeaked something terrible.

"Rebecca," Olive said. "It's like she read somewhere what a wife was supposed to do and then that's what she does. Like needlepoint."

"How long has she been around?" Mary climbed back on

the bed and set about unpacking the kit, picking her thread color and then trying to attach it to a long needle.

"Ici," Olive said, holding out her hand. "Give it to me, I'll thread it." She closed one eye and stuck her tongue through her teeth to focus and fed the eye of the needle with bright blue cotton. "She showed up years ago. I was down on the second floor then."

"This wasn't always your room?"

"Lord, no. I had my own rooms, near my father. The walls were yellow, and there was a chandelier that hung low right in the middle. It was a beautiful room." She sighed, handed the threaded needle back to Mary, and looked around. "Now I am up here with the other things the house outgrew."

"What about your father? He must miss you."

"He missed me before I was here. He missed me when I was right in front of him. He travels for work a lot. He told me that's why it was good Rebecca was coming to stay, that he was marrying her for me, for the manor."

Mary grimaced. "Sounds like true love. What are you making?" She leaned over to look at her cousin's hoop. Precise green leaves spiraled out from a circular tangle of vines and in the center were three letters—HTC. Olive was working small pink buds into the greenery.

"What does that stand for?"

"Henrietta Trudeau Craven," Olive answered without looking up. "My mother."

They worked in silence for a few minutes—Olive on her flowers and Mary trying to stitch a straight line without tangling her thread. "What was she like?"

"I don't know," Olive replied quietly. "She died when I was very young. Smallpox. Flora says that's why my dad went so mad about me, trying to keep me locked away, as if disease can be kept on the other side of a door." She gave a weak smile. "I didn't mind though. When I was young, that's when I would break out in hives at the thought of even going outside. Back then it wasn't so bad to stay in anyway. I was close to the rest of the house. Even had a cat."

"You did?" Mary was all ears. She had always wanted a pet. "Do you still have it?"

"No." Olive focused on her work, but there was a new tension in her voice. "Rebecca said it had to stay outside, that its fur made her sneeze and it would bring in sickness. I used to see it skulking around the backyard for a while, then one day it stopped coming."

"Do you think it found a new home?" Maybe she could find it, bring it back . . .

"I think the wolves found a new dinner," Olive answered glumly.

It was too horrible to comment on and Mary left it alone, even though she was dying to know if there were really wolves around here. They worked in silence until it became hard to see the stitches with tired eyes.

The next night, they decided to try out drama.

"Have you seen a play?" It was the first thing Olive said when Mary walked into the attic.

"I have," Mary answered. And she had, back when she was taken out of the house by Miss Patricks on Saturday afternoons so her mother could "rest." She often wondered what exactly her mother needed to rest from, but decided it was probably just her. Children have a hard time knowing when they're being louder than they need to be, and even when she tried tiptoeing and carefully tracing letters in her workbook, she was given the kind of looks that told her she was once again being disruptive.

"Oh, I knew it!" Olive stood on her bed and gave a quick bounce. She had been more active lately. Cutting back on her medicine seemed to be doing the trick, but Mary didn't comment on it. It stressed Olive out to acknowledge that she was defying orders and making her own decisions. "Tell me everything."

They sat on the Turkish rug in the center of the room, legs folded, facing each other. Mary dredged up every detail she could from the faded memory, filling in the blank spots with elaborate fables. Anything to entertain Olive.

"It was a warm night, and the theater was all lit up with white electric bulbs. You could see the marquee for miles around. The fancy people arrived in cars, wrapped in fur and the ladies wearing huge hats that were so heavy with flowers they had to be held with one hand or their necks would hurt. The men had waxed mustaches that curled, and one man had a small monkey on a leash that sat on his shoulder. It was very polite for a monkey and clapped at the appropriate moments. The mayor was there and he brought a princess with him as a date. I don't know where she was from, but she didn't speak English and her dress was made completely out of peacock feathers.

"We had seats in the second row from the front. The first row was set aside for the man with the monkey and the mayor with his royal guest and a bunch of other dignitaries who had financed the production. They were French and they drank champagne out of the princess's shoes. There were ushers running up and down the aisles like footmen, guiding old women in diamonds and carrying the heavy hats that had to be removed so that people in the back rows could see. They put them in the coatroom and, for a dollar, would water the flowers to make sure they didn't wilt before intermission.

"The curtains were red velvet, just as they're supposed to be, and the stage was so big you couldn't see all the way to the back without little binoculars. When it began, four men who worked at the circus lifting impossible weights pulled long ropes, and the curtains lifted, folding up into the rafters. After the applause quieted—the monkey was the last to stop clapping—the actors took the stage, dressed like medieval troubadours in brass-buttoned jackets and puffy pantaloons with tights and pointy shoes."

Olive was rapt, her eyes wide, her face cupped in her hands. "Oh, what play was it?"

"*Romeo and Juliet*," Mary answered. She knew that much was true. The rest was a blur. She had actually fallen asleep during that performance. It was a matinee, not an evening soiree, and as far as she could remember, there most certainly was no polite monkey or princess and nobody drank from anything other than a glass, but Olive was soaking it up. So she kept on going, detailing the set pieces, the full orchestra, and the way the actress playing Juliet seemed to float, so easily she glided across the stage in her lace and silks.

At the end of her story, which she finished off with a standing ovation that went on so long the theater threatened to call in the police if people didn't disperse, Olive stood and clapped. Mary obliged by curtsying.

"I want to do it!" Olive was flush with excitement.

"Do what?"

"Put on a play."

Mary sat back down. "But, Olive, how are we going to do a play? There's only two of us."

"We can each take on many parts. I'll be Juliet, of course, unless you want her, and you can be Romeo. What are the other roles?"

"I mean, their parents, Mercutio . . . but even still, we don't have costumes, or a stage, or an audience."

Olive was pacing now, thinking through the logistics.

"Maybe if we do it, if we practice our lines and get the movements right, maybe we can put it on for the manor. Maybe if my father sees how much better I feel, maybe he'll let me come back downstairs."

Mary understood this was about more than Shakespeare. This was about Olive making her grand entrance back onto the stage of life.

"Oh Mary, say you'll do it. Say you'll be my Romeo!" Olive was on her knees, hands clasped in the tight knot of prayer or begging, if they are actually different things. She looked like a little girl just then, her dark hair hanging around her face, her eyes filled with excited tears. How could she be denied anything?

"Of course I will," Mary agreed, filling with worry even as she said the words. She really wished she had paid more attention in that half-empty theater all those years ago. She didn't have much time to think about it because she was tackled by her cousin, who threw both arms around her in a massive hug that sent them both sprawling on the carpet.

Before she left that night, a little later than usual since Olive was too excited to sleep, Mary had decided she would have to search the house for a copy of the play. And she would have to start to think about telling Flora.

After all, if they were going to put on a production, she was going to need some help.

# 7

# A Dark Shadow Falls over the Bay

Like most days, now that Mary had found Olive, the day could not go quick enough. She had already found an excuse to get away from Flora and search her uncle's office for the Shakespeare book. Turns out he had a small collection of single play volumes on a lower shelf. She'd retrieved *Romeo and Juliet*, and it was already waiting in the drawer of her desk for later.

To fill the hours until evening when she could make a break for the attic, Mary went outside and looked for Jean.

The older man was on his knees pulling the new weeds that were cropping up around the greenhouse that held the vegetables. She cleared her throat. "Jean? I would like to be put to good use."

He turned his head slow, as if his neck was on a timed mechanism. He looked at her for a moment, then slowly turned back to his work. She waited.

"Well? Can I be of assistance?" Another moment passed before—

"Weeds all 'round the base," he finally said. "Greenhouses and gardens, too."

She clapped her hands. "Right then, I'll weed. Where would I find the equipment for that?"

He chuckled a bit before holding up both hands and wiggling his fingers.

"Surely there are at least gloves?" There was no way she was going to suffer the cuts and blisters that had turned his skin to a hard shell. "I don't want all that muck getting under my nails."

He pointed to the wheelbarrow parked by the greenhouse doors. She was still annoyed by his refusal to engage in proper conversation, but was starting to get used to it. So, she walked to the wheelbarrow and inside found a pair of stiff leather gloves and a small metal spade with a wooden handle. "These will do." She put the shovel in the pocket of the apron she had slipped over her dress and pulled on the gloves. They were much too big, leaving half the finger space empty and floppy, but they were better than nothing.

"I'll start on the gardens. You can manage the greenhouse areas," she instructed, as if Jean had been waiting for her command. He didn't even acknowledge her this time, so she made her way to the edge of the trees, where the first two gardens' walls showed through the branches.

"Seems a bit useless," she muttered. "Who cares about weeds around the gardens when the gardens are in the forest?" But still, it would kill time. So she carefully settled herself on the ground and began to dig and yank.

There was something satisfying about the work, a steady rhythm of the flex and pull of under-used muscles. The sun was doing its level best to evaporate all trace of energy through her skin. After an hour, she had shed both her apron and the sweater buttoned closed under that. She worked happily in her cotton dress, her legs tucked up under her. She was even humming, though she didn't notice, and couldn't have told what song it was had she been asked. When Flora called them in for lunch, Mary gulped down a glass of lemonade, poured a second and drank it between bites of a meat pie fresh from the oven. Then she was back out, leaving before Jean had even settled into his second slice.

The afternoon went quickly this way, digging and humming, moving from one patch to the next, and finally on to the second garden. She had a satisfyingly large pile of extricated weeds wilting on the side of the path. She knew they would grow back, would find ways to cling even harder, but that was part of the charm in the process—that it was not definite, that things would come back and change and that she could do it all again. Life was comfortable in its movements if you allowed it to be.

She was halfway done with the second garden when she came to the birch trees growing so close to the stone wall, they seemed to almost erupt out of it. Here there were a few patches of crabgrass, a short sapling dried to bone but rooted deep, and a couple of mushrooms.

"Ew," she muttered, pulling out the mushrooms and smushing them between her gloved fingers, not caring how much Philomene might have wanted them for supper. There were things she had grown used to seeing on her plate, but that, in the wild, seemed to be something else entirely, something to be avoided. Mushrooms were one of those things. She didn't even want to imagine how she might feel about meat if she were ever forced to hunt her own.

She yanked out the grass easily enough, but the sapling, which was now not much more than a stick, took some doing. She pulled so hard she had to leverage all her weight backward, and then her hands slipped. She fell solidly on her backside. Angry, she brushed the dirt off her skirts and stood, checking to make sure no one had witnessed her fall. Standing, she clapped her gloves together to clear off the dust, then grabbed the brush and yanked again until her head was thrown back and her neck was tense. She let it go and kicked at it with her leather shoes, one way, then the other. But the brush, a few branches now snapped off in the tussle, stood exactly as it had when she started.

"All right." She rolled up her sleeves, smearing mushroom remnants on the cotton. "I'll just have to unearth you, then." She picked up the small spade and began to dig.

Mary had never considered before just how rooted a thing could be, even a dead thing like this. She had no way of knowing how what she saw above the surface was mirrored underneath, the roots as long and twisty as the branches. The digging took longer than she had imagined, especially from having to stop and readjust to get around the woody roots that refused to be sliced through with something as flimsy as a garden spade. But she was determined. Now she was messy, caked in dirt and sweat, tired and achy, but more than all this, she was determined.

She had dug enough to pull half the structure up so that it leaned to the side now. She was working her way underneath, excavating a clear tunnel to the other side, nothing here but some small rocks and harder clay. And then the metal hit something larger, something that made a sound like a muffled bell.

"Damn stones," she cursed. She felt like the kind of person who would curse, looking like this, digging in the dirt like this, so she did it again. "Damn stones are damn well everywhere."

She tried to dig around it, but it was long. If it was a stone, it was an oddly shaped one. She scooped out mounds of dirt and snaked the tool back in and finally found an edge. Only it was just that—a squared edge and not a smooth curve like a rock should be. She slid the shovel's tip along the edge and came to a corner.

"What is this?"

She scooped out as much loose dirt as she could and then lowered both hands into the new hole, the gloves making it hard to maneuver. Without thinking, she pulled them off and threw them to the side, then dug back into the dirt with her bare hands. She grasped and wiggled and finally managed to pull out the object.

It was a small metal tin, long and shallow with two tiny hinges holding the top half to the bottom. The top was rusted so that the words that might have been there were obscured, but, brushing aside the dirt, Mary was able to make out the picture—a single red rose, faded to pink and chipped with rust, but in full bloom. When she tipped it over to examine the bottom, something inside rattled.

A treasure? She held her breath, not taking her eyes off the little box for a second. She sat back on her bottom, directly in the scrubby grass and finally released her breath.

Mary wasn't normally the kind of girl who got excited over treasure novels, stories about pirates or hidden ruins. Those tales were for children, and she was already a young woman. At least, she wasn't the kind of reader who would *admit* she got excited about them. But this? This was more than a story. This was an honest to God treasure box buried in a forest in a wild, dangerous land and she, Mary Craven, had unearthed it.

She wondered who had buried it here and when. Had they placed it under the small tree with careful hands, or had they planted the tree on top of it? Did Olive know about it? Had it been here before the house was built? Unable to put it off any longer, Mary decided to open it. She held the top in one hand, the bottom in the other, and pulled them apart . . .

But the rust had sealed it shut. She worked at it, the tip of her tongue poking out between her teeth, her heart beating against her ribs from exertion and excitement at the same time. She yanked and strained, then changed her grip and tried again. Finally, she retrieved the spade and tried to jam the blade under the rim of the lid. It budged a bit, making it uneven in the front, but still, it wouldn't open.

"Come on. Come on!" She turned it upside down on a flat rock and used both hands to push the spade tip in deeper. It squeaked a bit—metal on metal, but still, the box stayed closed. Mary was getting angry. She didn't like when things didn't immediately do as they were told. Things were supposed to be orderly and obedient, that's how it went.

From somewhere in the near distance she heard Flora call out. "Mary! Time to come in for tea!"

"Oh no, no, no, not now." She pulled the spade back and brought it down on the tin like a hammer. "Not now."

She didn't want Flora to come back here looking for her. This was *her* treasure. She didn't want to hand it over or even show it to anyone else, no one except Olive. It would be their secret together. They might make her hand it over, might insist that she stay out of the woods where private things were buried. It would become the property of adults, and she needed it to be hers. Too many things had been taken from her already.

"Jean, have you seen Mary?" Flora's voice was closer now.

Mary threw down the spade and looked around. She saw a large round stone near the birch trees and ran over to grab it. It had come loose from the garden wall and was heavy enough to do the trick. She carried it back and smashed the tin again. This time there was a loud crunch.

"Mary?"

She could hear Flora's footsteps now. Sweat stung her eyes and she had to keep one closed. She swiped at her cheek with the back of her hand, still carrying the heavy rock, and left a stripe of dirt on her skin. "Come on, come on . . ."

She called out, trying to sound nonchalant, trying to sound like a girl who was busy at work, who had simply lost track of time, who was not doing something secret in the woods. "Just a minute! Coming!"

*WHAM!* She hit the tin again, and this time it caught the

corner, and the little box went flying off the flat rock. It landed two feet away, onto the path, where Flora was right now walking into the woods. It bounced and, on the second tumble, came down on its side. The top split off and ricocheted into the bush. It was open!

"Mary, there you are."

"I'm coming now," Mary huffed. "Lord almighty, I was just finishing up. What's the rush?" She was used to reacting with anger, and those around her were used to being on the receiving end. The good thing about her moods is that they made people roll their eyes or want to move away from her, and Flora did both now.

Mary walked fast to join the older girl, stopping a foot away and bending down on one knee. "I just need to pull this prickly burr out of my stocking. Ugh! It's so horrible back here."

Flora turned her back on her, arms folded across her chest. "Well, I am so sorry, me, for bothering to come save you from this *horrible*."

Mary's eyes searched the ground—the bottom of the tin was upside down at the edge of the path and there, just by her shoe, was her treasure: a fancy filigree key on a faded pink ribbon. She jammed it into the waist of her skirt and took Flora's arm. She couldn't pretend to be annoyed anymore, not now that she had her prize.

"I'm just famished. I apologize for my tone. Thank you for

coming to get me. I hope there's lots of desserts," she sang, feeling every inch of her body alight and buzzing now that the secret key was safely in her possession.

Flora shook her head, muttering. "Crazy, I tell you. Crazy as the day is long. How do youse get anything done in the city with all that sass?"

---

Washed up and full of as much food as she could manage to eat in her state, Mary had left the dining room and was now lying on her bed, willing the sun to fall into slumber and take the rest of the house with it.

She had locked her bedroom door so she could have a moment to examine the key. She held it in her hand, twisting it in the late daylight that fell in a soft sheet over her bed warming her legs. There was hardly any rust on it, unlike the container that had kept it safe. And the ribbon was velvet, a quality fabric, thick and unfrayed but faded and obviously worn. She could see the wrinkles and indents where it had been pulled into a bow many years ago.

"What are you for?" she asked aloud. "Where do you belong?"

She had imagined a dozen things already—a chest buried somewhere along the shore left by pirates, one full of jewels or rare volumes. She imagined a locked room in the house where another girl had lived, or perhaps had died, one who wandered the floor in heavy velvet robes and whose hair once was held by this ribbon. She imagined a different house somewhere out in the bigger woods, a cottage where magic was practiced and jars held ingredients ranging from chunks of amber to reptilian eyeballs. She had even considered that perhaps it unlocked one of the drawers in Mr. Craven's massive desk, one that held secrets so horrible they would shock the entire territory.

But really, she knew—the same way she knew the moon was powerful when it was full and that her mother's final thoughts were not of her, she knew it as fact: This key unlocked the seventh garden. She wondered what could be in that garden that was so precious, or so dangerous, that it had to be locked away. She was imagining how many tigers could live behind those stone walls when her day of work in the hot sun finally caught up with her. Her eyes closed, the key falling lightly beside her on the quilt.

The dream was familiar right away. In it, the air was as warm as it had been today, but the quality of the light was different. It felt as if the entire sky was an electric bulb, like the one her mother had installed in the Toronto kitchen, and not a fiery sun. Sound was different, too, muffled, without echo or depth. It was like the entire yard was in a sealed container.

Once again, she was on a wooden swing hanging on thick rope from the low branch of the oak tree in her Toronto yard.

And then suddenly, there was the girl from next door swinging beside her. Although, this time, the swing was farther away, and in between them was a third swing, still and empty.

"My mother wouldn't be pleased," the girl said between giggles. "Wasting time like this."

"We've done this before," Mary answered.

"We have?"

"Yes, you're Brandy McCarthy and you live . . . used to live next door to me." Mary was saying the words but really, there were no memories attached to them. She knew them as facts, not events.

"I am?" The girl, who was indeed a version of Brandy, swung higher and higher, leaning back to pick up speed, smiling like crazy.

"Yes, and you do not like me." Again, another fact. No feeling.

"I don't?" Brandy was getting so high she was arching up into what looked dangerously like a full circle, all the way around the branch.

"You're going too high," Mary said, this time with feeling, and the feeling was fear. "You'd better slow down."

"But I don't want to," Brandy replied in a cadence that sounded like a song.

"You're going to hurt yourself!"

"Why do you care?" she asked. "We don't even like each other, you said."

"No, I like you, but you don't like me!" Mary was getting frantic. She could barely see the girl's face when she passed by. It was a blur of pale skin and white teeth.

"But why? Why do you like me?" Brandy was singing now for certain.

"Because I do! Because I want to be normal like you, have a brother like you. Have a life. A mother . . ."

"But why?" This time she spoke normally, and even more jarring, she was completely still, her feet planted in the grass beneath them. And she wasn't smiling anymore.

"Because . . . because I don't have a mother . . . anymore. Maybe I never did." Mary felt like crying. It was a hot tickle in her cheeks that made her blink fast. She hated this feeling. Her mother, when she was alive, would catch her blinking quick and scold her before the first tear ever fell.

*Mary Elizabeth Craven, are you crying? Ladies don't cry. Only toddlers do. Babies cry. Ladies hold it together. So if you are not a mewling infant, then I suggest you hold it together. Now!*

"Hey, why did you put this swing here?" Brandy sounded surprised. Had she not noticed it before now?

"I didn't put it here," Mary answered honestly.

"Yes you did. You put me here." Brandy kicked her feet out, ready to start climbing the air again.

"I did?"

"You did. This is all your doing," the girl said. "So why did you put this swing here? There's only two of us."

Mary was confused. She tried to stand up but couldn't; as soon as she tried, pins and needles shot into her legs, making her hiss.

"Are we expecting someone?" Brandy's voice was coming from up high. Mary didn't want to look, didn't want to watch the wildness of her movements. She liked order. She liked safety.

"I don't know."

"What do you mean you don't know? Did you invite someone else to join us?" Now the voice was coming from everywhere, the sky, the ground, her own head.

"No."

"I think you did. Someone else is on the way. Maybe they are coming down as we speak."

Down? Down from where? It was then that Mary thought of Olive. Maybe Olive was coming. If she had made a third swing appear, it could only have been for her cousin.

"It's Olive's!" she called out, and, truly speaking, allowing her physical voice to work, she woke up.

"Olive," she said her name again before the dream took the image and the name with it back into the ether. She was confused. She was fully dressed and on top of her blankets, but the sky outside was full dark.

"Oh God." She sat up quick, throwing her legs off the side of the bed. All she had wanted to do was waste the day so she could get back to the attic, and she had fallen asleep! "Olive . . ."

And then she remembered, and the memory skipped into her breath like a bubble: She had a secret. And while she couldn't share it with anyone lest it be taken away, she could share it with her captive cousin. She felt around in the dark until her fingers closed over the key. It was real. It was real and it was here, and she had to get to the attic and tell Olive all about it. Maybe she knew more about the garden and what secrets it held.

She fumbled around looking for matches in the dark and burnt her finger trying to light the lamp, but once she had it lit, she was back to her excitement. Leaving her shoes by the door, her hair still mussed from her long nap, she crossed the room on silent socks and threw open the door to the hallway.

The passageway was dark and there was no sound from downstairs. She worried she might have slept too long and that now Olive would be asleep. *Never mind*, she thought. Olive couldn't be mad at her, not once she heard her story and saw the key. She had just turned the first corner toward the doorway to the attic when she slammed directly into someone.

"Oh!" she cried out. It was all she could do to hold on to the lamp and not set the hall runner on fire.

"Where are you going at this hour?"

Mary lifted the lamp. This was not a voice she knew, and something about it made her guts pinch. Something about it reminded her of being told not to cry because ladies do not cry. They hold it together. So that's what she tried to do now.

The woman blocked the entire hallway, which seemed impossible as she was tall and thin, as thin as anyone Mary had ever seen. But something about her presence was a blockade. Her hair was all blond ringlets, piled up in strange shapes, and at her throat, the flame in the lamp caught the dazzle of jewels. Her dress was still bustled, and her back was very straight. And then Mary knew exactly who this was.

Rebecca Craven.

Olive's stepmother was home.

# 8

# The Aunt Issue

Rebecca Craven had perfect posture. From around her long neck hung several necklaces at a time. It was an extravagance to begin with but especially more so since she had to have her high collars tailored down to facilitate the chains. Mary could tell she liked people to know she was the kind of woman who could wear delicate jewelry even in a rustic setting, several pieces at once, and also that she was the kind of woman who could afford to get her collars altered for that very reason. She might have called herself proud, but some people had another way to describe it.

On that first night, Olive had told Mary all about her.

*"She'd take the cross from the Jesus if he'd put it down for a moment,"*

Olive had told her. *"Everything is about her. I wonder if she even knows my middle name."*

*"What is it? Your middle name?"*

*"Niiganigiizhig,"* she had answered. *"It was one of my granny's names."*

*"Your grandma was a real Indian?"* Mary had blurted.

*"As opposed to what? A false one?"* Olive had challenged her, but not unkindly. Even stashed in the attic with the other forgotten things, she was accustomed to this line of questioning, as she explained to Mary. *"My mother was a Drummond Islander, one of the Ojibwe half-breeds who came over after the American war. Both her parents were half-breeds, too—both spoke the strange kind of French they all did. At some point, we became our own people."*

*"Oh."* Mary had felt sheepish then, but rallied when she remembered where she had heard of that place before. *"Drummond Island. That's where Flora's Père came from, too."*

*"There's lots of us here. Once, there was only us—Indigenous people who were already here, and the newcomers like us. There were some soldiers around, too, and the very few families who were trying to start the lumber trade. My father's family was one of them. He's English."*

*"I know, silly,"* Mary had teased. *"He's my family, too."*

*"Right, right . . ."* Olive had murmured. *"Sorry, I have to get used to having real family."*

*"Real family?"*

*"My father is always gone. And Rebecca is not real family,"* Olive had said. *"She's something else entirely."*

"I assume you are the orphaned niece?" the woman asked, but it felt like more of an assessment than a question.

"I am." Mary tried to stand her ground, but she was so shocked at having been discovered, she was finding it hard to make eye contact.

She placed her bony hands on her hips. "Well then, I'm sure the servants let you run wild, but in this home, when we go to bed, we stay in bed."

Mary ventured a look at the woman's face. It was half in shadows, but the scowl was very visible. "Yes. All right." She turned and walked back to her room.

Rebecca Craven stood where she had stopped and watched her progression, as if she were a wall rather than a woman.

---

The next day, the house was already different. And by dinner, Mary decided she hated her aunt Rebecca. Not only was she rude to Flora and Philomene, but she refused to even allow Jean in the house.

"Why does he even have to come inside? His work is entirely out of doors and so that's where he should remain." She had this way of wrinkling up her nose when she spoke about Jean that reminded Mary of a pig's snout.

The woman stayed upstairs in her rooms for the entirety of the morning, only coming down to unleash her disapproval on the staff and pointedly ignore Mary. When she descended at lunch, ready to give new commands, she acted as if everyone else had spent the morning lazing about.

"I want this entire place dusted, all the wood oiled, and a complete inventory of the pantry and storerooms," she barked, swirling into the dining room in layers of bright pink cotton skirts.

"We dust every second day," Flora said. She had just finished laying out lunch for Mary, who was seated by the window, deep in thought about the Olive situation. She jumped when her aunt spoke, as if she had been plotting out loud and had just been caught.

"Are you talking back?" Rebecca stood very still, waiting for Flora's answer, hands on her hips.

"No, Madame . . ."

"Then go get your things and begin your chores. I don't think this one small girl needs a dedicated maid to eat lunch, do you, Mary?" She turned her attention to the girl, who sat up straighter—an automatic response she'd developed over the years under the intermittent scrutiny of her own mother.

"No, ma'am."

The woman sighed, lowering herself carefully into one of the seats and pouring a black tea, no milk, no sugar. "Aunt Rebecca."

Mary looked at her blankly.

"You are to call me Aunt Rebecca," the woman repeated, forcing a small smile. "I am your uncle's wife, and I am to be addressed in the same way his former wife would have been." Her face pinched at the mention of the first Mrs. Craven. She covered it by lifting her teacup and taking a sip. "I am the woman of this house. Always will be."

The second part was said more to herself, low and heavy. It made Mary think of Olive just then, alone in the attic. Funny, sweet Olive, so small in that big bed, her own blood cousin wasting away under the rafters.

"Say it."

Mary blinked. "Pardon?"

"Say it," the woman repeated, her eyes gone dark and unmoving.

And for a moment, Mary was confused. What was she to say? She folded her hands in her lap and swallowed hard.

"*Say my name.*" This was punctuated at the end with a palm slapping the tabletop, making the silver cutlery clatter.

"A-Aunt Rebecca?"

Like a candle had been lit, Rebecca's face brightened. Her eyes came alive, her hands resting daintily around her porcelain cup. "Yes, dear. That's nice now, isn't it?" She spoke at a higher octave, her lips moving into a smile that didn't quite fit her smooth face, her head tilted slightly to the side. She didn't wait for an answer. Instead she called for Flora, who came quickly, but without her signature mirth.

"Yes, Madame?"

"Remove all . . . this . . ." She indicated the lunch spread by wiggling her extended fingers, as if it were something uncouth. Flora and Philomene had in fact gone out of their way today to set out freshly baked scones, cured ham, a potato salad with scallions and dill from the kitchen window herb garden, and small drops of meringue glazed with wild honey. It was a feast not only in taste but for the eyes. It was obvious the women had gone above and beyond for their mistress's first lunch since she'd been back.

Mary felt her stormy temper begin to flare.

"I won't be taking lunch: I'm on a new nutrition regime," Rebecca proclaimed with a sniff of pride. "And my lovely niece should also be adjusting her intake. She will have fresh berries for breakfast, milk and boiled eggs for lunch, and a plate of sliced beef for dinner."

"I don't like milk," Mary said. She certainly wasn't going to have this woman deciding what she could and could not eat.

Rebecca sighed. "You may not know this, dear, but my brother is a medical doctor. He even went to England for some of his training. I have asked him for guidance on what to consume, and he has given me the benefit of his wisdom for everyone in this house. And, as the woman of the manor, I am responsible for your well-being. All of us." Her tone didn't quite match up with the words, so the entire statement came out like a kind of warning.

"Does he take care of Olive?"

Mary said it like a challenge and caught Flora's response—eyes rounded, mouth agape. It was the first she'd heard that Mary knew about the prisoner in the attic.

"As a matter of fact," Rebecca said smoothly, as if dealing with petulant children were the most boring task of her day, "he is Olive's main doctor. That's how I first came to know Mr. Craven. And he'll be yours, too. And I think right about now he would say your nerves are on edge, indicating the need for some time alone in your room."

Mary stayed seated, her eyes locked on her aunt, who kept her gaze level on the girl. Flora stood in the doorway like a pedestrian just trying to get to the saloon while a gunslinger showdown was taking place on the main street of a Western town.

After a few long, heavy beats of silence, it was Rebecca who spoke again. "You know, perhaps we should start delegating times that you should remain in your room if you are this unsettled here. I can keep the door locked if it would help calm you in these new surroundings."

Mary knew when she was bested. She pushed back her chair so quickly that it scraped the floor, the sound making

Rebecca close her eyes in exasperation. Then she stood, tossed her napkin on the table, and walked to the doorway.

"Aren't you forgetting something?" Rebecca simpered.

Mary was in front of Flora, her back to her aunt when she spoke. What could she be forgetting? She just wanted to leave, to get away from this horrible woman, to go to her room and start a new list, perhaps titled *Ways to Defeat an Evil Step-Aunt.*

Flora cleared her throat softly and, when she caught the girl's eye, she tapped her own cheek and motioned with her lips to the table behind them. Mary sighed, deep and heavy, turned on a heel, and marched back to the table. She bent and placed a small, quick kiss on the woman's cheek. Her skin smelled of roses and something else—something medicinal. Camphor, maybe?

"That's better," Rebecca cooed, happy now that her victory had been secured with the humiliation of a teenager having to provide a child's kiss. "We'll see you in one hour, then, after you've sorted yourself out."

It took everything in her not to scream. When Mary got to her room with the door closed behind her and her face buried in a pillow, that's exactly what she did. How could this woman come into the house and treat everyone so horribly? Who exactly did she think she was?

It occurred to Mary then that this was exactly the way her own mother had been—demanding, and more than that, demeaning. Mary herself had walked into the manor with the same kind of attitude. She blushed thinking of the way she had acted when she first arrived. She may have not held Miss Patricks in the same regard as say Flora or Philomene, but had that woman deserved that kind of treatment?

*No use putting worry into the past. It can't fix anything*, Flora had told Mary one morning when she was lamenting leaving her silver-handled brush back in the Toronto house. *Best to look ahead when you step.*

And so Mary got up, fixed her rumpled dress, and set out on a mission.

---

She might have been caught on her last nighttime journey, but now Rebecca was busy on the first floor; she could hear her conducting a complete rearrangement of the living room when she opened her door a crack. Mary pulled off her shoes and, closing the door behind her, set off for the narrow staircase that would take her to Olive.

In the daylight, the journey seemed half as long. Without shadows, the walk could be taken at a brisker pace with no chance of barking a shin or stubbing a toe. And, if she were being honest, with a well-lit path, there were fewer places for terrible things to hide.

She got to the staircase, climbed carefully so as not to let the old wood creak too much, and finally stood at the closed door at the top.

She turned the knob but it wouldn't give.

She tried again, twisting it the other way. Nothing. Locked!

Mary knocked quietly, pushing her face up against the crack in the wood. "Olive," she whispered. "Olive, are you there?"

Silence.

She knocked louder. "Olive, it's me, Mary."

She put her ear against the wood but couldn't hear anything.

Remembering how big the space was, Mary knew she'd have to give a hell of a loud bang to be heard all the way over to the bed, and that was only if her cousin was awake. But that kind of a knock could summon Rebecca from downstairs.

After a few more tries, Mary went back to her room, pulled out her borrowed paper and ink, and sat down to write a letter.

*Dearest Cousin Olive,*

*I came to see you last night, but your stepmother came home and caught me in the hallway. I haven't forgotten about you. I never will. I am going to try to come to you again this evening and every evening after for as long as it takes.*

*In the meanwhile, I think you should eat the good food Flora prepares (though I am starting to think that food might be eggs and milk—yuck) and open the windows where you can in order to allow in the nice air. Despite your fearful thoughts, there is nothing in the sky or on this land that I have found to be detrimental. And make sure you get out of bed as much as you can. Flora says a brisk walk can do wonders, and I trust her more than any other counsel to be found up here. I suspect Philomene and Jean would also have good advice, but I've yet to get them speaking more than a few words at a time.*

*You are forever in my thoughts.*

*Love, your adoring cousin,*

Mary Craven

*PS: I have a very big secret to tell you, but I want to do it in person so I can see your lovely face when you hear it!*

*PPS: Have you heard about Flora's sister Sophie? I am torn to bits with curiosity about her. Can a girl really run through the woods in pants and climb trees like a clawed thing? Can such a girl exist in this world? I must know if you've met her. If I know such a character is real, I might feel different about the entirety of life!*

When she was done writing, she added a quick sketch of a small trillium flower beside her signature and folded the page neatly, making sure to press down on the edges, and then penned *OLIVE CRAVEN* on the back in her best calligraphy.

Mary was bursting to tell Olive about the key, about the

seventh garden, about the secret they would share. Right now, the key was pushed under the back corner of the rug, up against the back wall of Mary's bedroom. Since Rebecca's arrival, Mary was jittery about its location, checking on it twice before breakfast. Now more than ever she needed this small, bright trinket, this doorway into something else, somewhere else. She wanted it to be a place for only her and Olive, and this letter was the first step in subverting her aunt's authority over them.

She slid it under the door at the top of the stairs and then stood back. Mustering all her courage, she lifted both fists and banged on the door as if there were an emergency. The sound echoed in the stairwell. She didn't wait for a response; instead she picked up her skirts and ran down the steps, up the hall, and into her room, only slowing down to quietly close her door.

Not two minutes later, Rebecca opened it back up.

"What is going on here?" Her eyes darted all around the room and landed on Mary, holding up one side of her wooden dresser.

"Oh, sorry, Aunt Rebecca. I just wanted to move around the room a bit. You know, freshen up and clean under furniture, maybe rearrange a few things." She made a show of dropping the dresser so that it landed with a bang. "Sorry if I was being loud. I'll try to be more careful."

Rebecca stood, eyes narrowed, for a moment. She had

come up to yell, that much was clear. Had maybe even *wanted* to yell. But catching the girl doing what she herself was doing downstairs was a hard thing to be mad about. So she cleared her throat. "Yes, well. Wait for staff to assist. Don't be damaging this furniture. It's very costly, you know."

"I know," Mary agreed. "I'll wait, then."

When the woman left and she was once again alone, Mary plopped down on her bed and smiled.

---

Flora showed up with a tray several hours later. Mary was sprawled on her bed reading *Jane Eyre*, her stockinged feet resting on her pillow.

"She sent up your dinner," Flora said, placing the tray on the desk. "Says you should take it here. Though you're not missing much by not joining her, let me tell you."

Mary bent the page she was on and closed the book, pulling herself to a sitting position. "Flora, why didn't you tell me about Olive?"

Flora's cheeks flushed and for a moment it looked like she was going to rush out. Instead, she sat down in the chair. "Oh Mary. I wanted to. I swear to the Jesus I did. But Rebecca said no, you weren't to know. Weren't to go up there all fulla piss and vinegar getting Olive all sick. In case you didn't notice for yourself, your aunt, she's none too pleased about you being here."

Mary scoffed. "Yes, she doesn't hide it well. But Olive is my cousin. My honest-to-God cousin. And she doesn't seem that sick to me, Flora. What's wrong with her exactly?"

"Well now, that depends on who you ask."

"I'm asking you."

"Okay, then, Miss Mary, if you ask me, she's cooped up like a wild animal in a pen and needs to be let out or she'll pine away to nothing," Flora answered, genuine distress on her face. "Her mother passed when she was just new, that one. And her father? He didn't know how to handle her—how to handle himself, really. Kept her inside, kept her put away. Like she was made of glass. Like the wind would blow her away. Couldn't handle any more loss. Hattie? She was his big love. She was everything. The only reason he got remarried is when the priest came by and told him he should, that it would be best for his little bébé."

"How did he meet Rebecca?"

"Oh, that one, well now . . ." Flora leaned in conspiratorially. "You know that brother she's so proud of, there? The one that studied in England? First of all, he went to London, Ontario, not London, England. Ha! Big difference. He was the girl's doctor. It was him that brought his sister over, like bait to fish, I think."

Mary put her hand over her mouth. "No!"

"Oh, oui!" Mary continued. "And it's no mistake neither. Your uncle, he's a rich man, and Rebecca, her family was ruined when the fur trade went belly-up, there. I think she brings her doctor brother around a little too much, me. I think your uncle and poor Olive are the only way he pays his bills."

"*Flora!*" Rebecca yelled up the stairs.

"Ah shit. I've gotta go," Flora said, standing up quick. "You just hold on there—tomorrow will be a better day." She stopped by the desk and began unloading a stash from her apron pockets all wrapped in cloth—slices of bread, a cold pat of butter, a cored apple, and several ginger cookies still warm from the oven. She winked at Mary, then rushed out the door.

Mary wondered why she would've had to carry up dinner in her pockets. But looking at the tray, she understood: a small plate of thinly sliced beef—that's it. No gravy, no side dishes, no salt. Rebecca's tenure over the house had truly begun.

Mary went to bed early, wondering if Olive got the letter. She heard Rebecca walking the halls and imagined she was a prisoner under guard. She tried to imagine all the ways tomorrow could be better, like Flora had suggested, and began to drift off. She wondered if Flora's siblings were tucked into bed yet, if they had been kissed by a loving mother and fed a good meal. She especially wondered about the mysterious Sophie. Did she even sleep in a bed? She thought perhaps that a creature like Sophie would be sleeping under the stars or maybe even on the roof of their cabin, with a hat pulled down over her eyes. Her thoughts gently turned back to her own predicament, and she almost giggled herself awake at the image of the wind catching under her skirts and her aunt Rebecca blowing up and over the house and into the sky, never to be seen again.

# 9

# Tomorrow Gets Better

The next morning, Flora woke Mary up an hour earlier than usual.

"Get up now, before the madame does. If you get ready, you can leave without her seeing."

Mary was confused but sat up anyway. "What's going on?"

"Shhh, now. Get dressed. I think she might make it in today. I sent word yesterday and if she's around, she'll most likely show up while there's still dew on the grass." Flora slipped out of the room, leaving Mary to wonder just who this "she" was who had been sent for.

Soon, she was dressed, had eaten a hasty bowl of oats, and was waiting by the dining room window for Sophie Beausoleil to arrive.

Sophie was taller than Mary but still short in the rest of the world. Here, she was average, maybe even a bit ahead of the scale. Flora had told Mary once that the people who were from the Bay were smaller because they were descended from voyagers, the men who portaged the country and carried massive weight on their shoulders and heads, which made them short and compact over the years. Mary wasn't sure that was a real thing, but she did notice the median height here was less than impressive. Even old Jean barely cleared five-foot-two, but he was wide and strong.

But it wasn't her height that made Sophie stand out. Maybe it was the way she stood, straight and with one hip slightly thrown back, as if she were about to sprint off. Maybe it was the way she dressed. On that day, she was wearing wool trousers, thin leather suspenders, and a man's white dress shirt with the sleeves folded up and the collar unbuttoned. Her face was definitely unique—narrow brown eyes, no eyebrows to speak of, full lips, and a sprinkling of small, dark freckles across her nose. She wore her hair pulled into two long braids that hung down her back with an old man's belled top hat pushed back from her forehead. Really, Mary thought it was all these things, these disparate and eclectic pieces pulled together, that made Sophie such a wonder.

Later, after they had become close, after the afternoons spent running in the woods and the canoe trips out on the Bay, in the days after they had spoken words they could not take back, Mary would know that all these things were secondary to the true wonder of the girl. That these things were only the doorway into a world she would live and die for, even at fifteen.

But that would come later. Today, all she had to go on in this first sighting of Sophie were these physical details, and she took them all in silently, watching from a safe distance in the dining room window as Sophie made her way up the backyard with a small crow sitting on her shoulder.

---

"Mary Craven, I would like to introduce you to my sister, Sophie Frederic Beausoleil." Flora gave a slight bow at the waist as if she were a footman announcing a royal visitor. They were all on the back lawn, close enough to the house to be shaded in its looming shadow.

"As if." Sophie laughed. "We're not at some fancy ball." She stepped forward and held out a hand to Mary, who hesitated before extending her own. "I'm pleased to make your acquaintance. And before you ask, 'cause they always surely do, yes, I have a man's name as my own middle name. I'm named Sophie for a grandmother and Frederic for a grandfather." She gave Mary's hand a good pump before stepping back. Released from the girl's grip, Mary's arm fell like an uncooked noodle and slapped against her skirt. "Flora tells me you've been here for almost two weeks now?"

Mary just blinked. She started to feel constricted, as if she were wearing a dress with a tight collar. And then, a remembered dread. Mary did not do well with things that amazed her. She was used to being ignored, misunderstood, small. But this girl? This girl was used to everything—wide open and full-on. So she did the only thing she could do in that moment to remain standing—she looked away.

If Sophie noticed, she didn't remark on it. She just kept talking. "Jesus, that's forever, especially in this fine weather! So then, you must have found the old fort, you?"

Mary shook her head.

"No? You haven't found the fort?" She looked shocked. "Come on, then." She paused, looking at Mary's white dress and shiny sandals. "Uh, I'll wait while you get changed. Pants would be best."

"I don't have pants," Mary answered. She was taken aback by the request but didn't mean to sound as shocked as she was, spitting out the word *pants* as if it were a curse.

"Well then, your worst best dress, I suppose. You really should get some pants though. Especially since we're gonna be exploring." As if to demonstrate the utility of her clothing, Sophie turned cartwheels down the lawn, legs splayed out above her head. The crow that had settled in a nearby tree cawed at her as if applauding.

Flora clapped her hands. "Oh Sophie, always on an adventure." Then she turned to Mary and shooed her inside. "Go on then, find something to put on. I'll see about getting some of your uncle's castoffs for later. We can always tailor them down for you. But for now, maybe the blue dress? The one that needs the hem fixed."

For a moment, Mary didn't move. Instead she watched Sophie, who was still turning cartwheels down the grass. Now the crow was flying in close, tapping the soles of her shoes when it came up before flapping back.

"Hurry, you!" Flora slapped Mary's leg with the dish-cloth she seemed to keep tucked into her apron for just this purpose.

She turned slowly, then walked back into the hall, through the mudroom, and into the kitchen. Philomene sat at the kitchen table peeling potatoes. She gave Mary a slight nod and went back to her work.

By the time she reached the bottom of the stairs, Mary got a sudden kick of adrenaline. She was going out on an adventure to find a fort with Sophie. She ran up the stairs as fast as she could in her ridiculous dress. Why shouldn't she have pants?

Why would any girl wear anything but pants? She could barely lift her foot to climb the next step, and here was Sophie doing acrobatics in the yard.

She sped down the hall to her room and slammed the door behind her, her heart in her ears. She struggled to get out of her layers, stripping down to a linen slip and underclothing. She went to her closet and grabbed the navy dress. Suddenly she couldn't move fast enough. The buttons took too long. The belt was too fussy. She managed to pull it on, and at the last minute decided against hosiery. She was still young—there was no big issue with her legs being bare, so she left them that way. It gave her a delicious feeling of freedom, though she did still wish she could pull on trousers. She hoped Flora would be true to her word and find her some. She didn't care if they were too big or out of fashion. She would wear them just the same. Maybe she could get a pair of suspenders, like the ones Sophie had.

She was about to run out when a sudden urge took her: She needed to have the key on her for safe-keeping. What if Rebecca came snooping around her room once she was gone? Without access to Olive, the key was all she had of her own, her one bright spot.

Mary crawled along the floor and lifted the corner of the rug, relieved to see the little brass key lying where she had left it. She wasn't sure why she thought it might be gone. *Maybe,* she thought, *this is what happens when you have something to lose—you become afraid*. She picked it up and dropped it into the small pocket sewn into her waistband.

There was a knock at her door. She opened it, expecting it to be Flora telling her to hurry. "I'm coming, I'm coming, hold your—"

"Hold my what?" Rebecca demanded. Her face settled into a deep frown, the lines around her mouth mirrored on her forehead.

Mary's mouth went dry. There was something about this woman that made her deeply troubled. Not afraid, not really, but troubled. Like the feeling one gets when they are still miles from home and the sky gets suddenly dark.

"Oh, sorry, Mrs. Craven—"

"Aunt Rebecca," she corrected. What should have been a sweet request to claim family sounded sharp and menacing in her voice.

"Sorry, Aunt . . . Rebecca. I was just headed back downstairs. I thought perhaps you were Flora."

"Why would Flora be up here on the second floor without being summoned?" Rebecca wrinkled her nose, and Mary thought of her mother, the way she insisted the staff be kept at a distance until they were called forth. "And why on earth are you slamming doors and stomping up the stairs?"

"I was . . . I was just trying to get ready to go outside."

"Outside? Why would you be going outside? And what is this you're wearing?"

Mary clenched her teeth. Rebecca was already keeping her from Olive—she wasn't about to let the woman stand between her and Sophie. She decided to bet on Rebecca's snobbery about city things and real ladies to get her out of this. "It's my old dress. I put it on so that I could go and help in the gardens. My mother, who was a part of the Toronto Horticulture League, always said a civilized lady must learn about plants from a young age. So that you can direct florists with knowledge."

Rebecca sniffed. "Well, of course, I know that. I myself am very adept at identifying breeds of roses."

Mary almost corrected her on her use of the term *breed* but bit her tongue. "Of course you are, Aunt Rebecca. I just want to one day be as capable as you."

"Well." Rebecca backed away from the door. "Don't let me hear you storming about the manor like a boy again. We cannot disturb Olive. She needs all the rest she can get. Now, go tend to the gardens. And, for goodness' sake, don't track any dirt inside. It's filthy enough as it is up here."

"Oh, thank you, Aunt. I will clean off in the kitchen on the way in." Mary slipped back in her room for her gloves (which would stay in her pocket for the rest of the afternoon) and slid past her aunt, making sure to take her time on the stairs.

"We need to talk soon, about your schooling," Rebecca called after her.

Mary didn't answer and chose to ignore the comment. Who could think about school when you lived out in the wild?

When Mary got to the kitchen door, she broke out in a run that carried her past Philomene. The old woman didn't look up this time, but chuckled softly to herself at the sudden energy in the sullen city girl who now flew out the back door like a bird out an open cage door.

# 10

# The Old Fort and a New Hideout

"I KNOW THESE LANDS LIKE THE BACK OF MY HAND," SOPHIE said, then held out both hands and turned them front to back. "Why do we say that, anyway? How well can you know the back of your hand, eh?"

She had been chattering like this since they left the yard and entered the woods. As they walked, she whistled and stopped now and then to pick up random sticks and plants, examine them, and then either toss them aside or slip them into her pocket.

It was good that Flora had sprung the visit on Mary, otherwise she wouldn't have slept. Since hearing about Sophie, Mary had built her up to legend status in her head. She was like a heroine from a storybook—someone who could talk with animals, decipher the wind movements, build fires, and track prey.

As it turned out, Sophie really could do most of those things in some capacity. Mary often found herself without words, but no matter; Sophie filled all the spots that would have been awkward with chatter. And not useless chatter, not about dress hemlines or polite table settings. Instead, she talked about her Père taking on the rapids in his light birchbark canoe, about the ways beavers change the landscape, and how the town was turning the cedar swamps into friendly harbors with gravel and sand. Important things that one needed to know if living in this place.

And then she asked Mary an important question, one the girl hadn't considered at all.

"Will you be staying here, then?"

Mary was silent, not for lack of words, but for lack of a decision. Would she stay? She was already fifteen, and marriage couldn't be far off. But then, who would she marry? She was an orphan. And though her uncle was wealthy, and she herself had money in a trust, which family would want to bring her into their fold? Would she be stuck marrying a logger or a lumber foreman up here? Would she return to the city to finish schooling and perhaps meet someone suitable there? She didn't even like most people. How would she find a man she could tolerate enough to share a home with?

"I don't know who I would marry," she finally answered.

Sophie, who had been checking a bush for signs of early berries, turned, letting the branches snap back. "Marry? How the Jesus did you get there, you? I didn't ask about that. I asked what you want to do, where you want to live. How you want to live."

It occurred to Mary for the first time that perhaps those things could be separate. There was a strange feeling in her muscles then, as if she were discovering some of them for the first time. Like there were more movements she could make.

"I . . . I don't know. I don't really know much about this place." She was pacing in a circle.

"And what do you know about the city?" Sophie wasn't being unkind; she was genuinely curious. It was this easy tone that took down Mary's defenses, that made her really think about it.

Finally, she stood still and sighed. "Not much."

"Well then." Sophie walked over and hooked an arm through Mary's, which made her jump. She wasn't accustomed to physical contact. "Let me tell you all about here. Huh, I can tell you lots about this place, me."

Sophie took Mary deeper into the woods, cutting east off the path that would lead them to the water, where Mary had picnicked with Jean and Flora.

"Some kids, maybe. That's who made this thing. I'm not so sure though. Could have been soldiers, or maybe the first ones that came from Drummond Island when Americans took it over and sent my people here," Sophie explained. "You'll see. It's very old. Hard to tell if it's a playhouse or a wrecked house. Maybe a temporary one, without a hearth, just a fire outside for cooking and that."

They were pushing through the low pine branches that clawed at their hair and scraped at their knees.

"How did you find it? It's pretty wild out here," Mary huffed. She was trying to keep up, both in pace and in good spirits, but it was hard. There were more blackflies out here, and she had already slapped herself in the face twice to stop a bite.

"Wild? Here?" Sophie looked back. "Ha! It's tame here. I don't hunt here, even. Too many people. The manor, the new docks going in just up the road from youse. One day, maybe, I'll show you *wild*."

Something about this, the idea of being in the wide unknown with this strong girl, made Mary feel excited instead of scared. If anyone could take her into the wild and come back alive, it would be Sophie.

The first signs of the Old Fort were felled and split logs seemingly dumped at different spots. It was hard to see them before they tripped you; the ferns here were lush and thick, growing like a carpet over the clearing.

"How long has this been here?" Mary wasn't even sure what "it" was yet.

"Oh, it's been abandoned since I was around. We have stories about the place—what it is, when it was put up. But my Père, he was sure it used to be a house, but he didn't know which family used it, so who knows."

"A whole family home?" Mary imagined the manor. How long would it take a structure like that to crumble and be eaten by the woods?

"Not a real house, a temporary shelter. Like the ones the Island people used when they first arrived, before they built the settlement."

Pushing through a line of cedars, they came to an old homestead. But it was unlike any home Mary had ever seen before. She wasn't sure what she was expecting. Stone maybe. Some sort of multiroom structure. But what was there was barely the size of a shed. It wasn't even near the size of one of the greenhouses back at the manor.

"It's a half-size house," she remarked, a bit disappointed.

"Close," Sophie answered, walking ahead. "It's a half-breed house." She laughed a bit, and it was clear to Mary that she had some nostalgia about this place. She shut her mouth about how underwhelming it was, how flimsy the roof was that it had already caved in, how inefficient the paneless window hole and rickety remaining walls looked.

Sophie waved her on, walking around the dangerously leaning back wall. "Anyway, this is the best part here!"

"Wait," Mary called, picking up her skirts and running.

Something about the thought of abandonment made her skin prick up in goose bumps. "I don't think we should go in. That wall looks like it's gonna fall. Sophie?"

There was no answer, but they did not go inside. Instead, Mary found Sophie in the back standing on a small platform, surrounded by a semicircle of apple trees bursting in flower.

"Wow, those are pretty."

"When the fruit comes, we'll come back and pick them, armfuls, enough for jam in the cold months," Sophie said cheerfully. "My mother, she makes the best pies, you cannot even imagine. But that's not the best thing—this is." She jumped up and down on the wood. It groaned under her weight but barely moved.

"That?" Mary approached skeptically. Maybe she was missing something. "What is that? A floor?"

"It's a stage, mon ami! A real live stage!" And then she broke out in a little dance, a kind of tap dance that she exaggerated by spinning her arms madly in opposite directions. The spectacle of her, her hat pushed at a jaunty angle, one suspender slipping down her arm, her tongue pushed out in mock concentration, made Mary laugh and clap.

"But why? Why is there a stage here, at this shack?"

Sophie sat on the edge of the platform, catching her breath. "Dieu, if you think this is a shack, you better not come to my place."

Mary felt ashamed, but Sophie covered it up with a little

chuckle. She seemed incapable of holding any hard feelings. "Because, the life of the family is not about how many chairs you can fit around the table, it's how many bodies can fit in the yard. They probably used this for dancing and fiddling, or maybe for telling stories. But we can use it for whatever we want."

Mary thought about it. There was always something about the theater that made her excited. The costumes, the lights, and the bodies gliding so effortlessly and in quick choreography with one another held her attention completely.

"Maybe we can do an opera?" She said it softly, timid to bring up her own idea. She couldn't help but picture Olive's face in the front row, beaming, healthy, or maybe even onstage with them in a grand dress or a tailored soldier's coat.

"Yes!" Sophie leapt to her feet. "I have no idea what an opera could be, but yes! We will do it!"

The crow, who had just landed on her shoulder, burst back into the air with an indignant squawk at her sudden animation and sat complaining about it in one of the apple trees.

---

They went to the shore next, where Sophie instructed Mary on the best stones to skip—flat and light, but with enough weight to pick up speed. Mary was a dismal failure at it, but she did enjoy tossing rocks into the lake. There was something satisfying about the abandon of a good throw, about the disruption of a smooth surface with a small projectile of chaos.

Sophie told her about driftwood and ice fishing and about the islands that dotted this water like a broken string of pearls. "Some are as big as a man lying flat," she insisted. "Others are miles and miles of birch and willow and rocks stacked like crepes."

"I can't believe it . . ." Mary was flushed. She had taken off the cardigan she'd grabbed on her way through the mudroom and wrapped it around her waist. Her hair had fallen loose and curled damp at her temples. She stumbled a bit on the rocky shoreline. They'd left the sandy beach and were walking toward where the trees met the water on the western edge of the clearing.

"You have to learn how to step," Sophie said, pointing to Mary's feet with a tilt of her chin.

"How to step? What do you mean?"

"The rocks." Sophie jumped from one large rock to another, then scampered over the smaller stones. The sound was like bubbles popping. "You have to know how to move with the land, not against it. Not everything is a fight. Sometimes it's like . . . a dance." She jumped onto a grassy knoll and spun with a small flourish, her hands above her head.

They both laughed at this absolute balletic movement. Mary felt like it was the loudest sound she'd ever made—this laughter, with this girl, on this beach. But with a thought, she suddenly grew serious.

"Sophie?"

"Oui?"

"Can you keep a secret?"

Now they had both stopped laughing and spinning and stood still, looking at each other in the bright clear of the Georgian Bay morning.

---

"This door hasn't been opened in years, not since poor Hattie passed on," Sophie was whispering even though they were the only souls in the woods. "My mother, she told me about it. And of course, I've seen it here. But never thought . . ."

"It could be opened again?" Mary finished in a low voice, almost a whisper, though she didn't know why, except that this place was the closest she'd ever felt to being in church in years. She pulled out the key from her pocket and held it up between them.

"Where did you get that?"

"I dug it up in an old tin." Mary pointed off toward the path. "Outside one of the other gardens."

"And my sister, does she know you have it?" Sophie turned to her. Mary caught her breath in that gaze. She didn't want to answer wrong. This had been the most perfect day so far. She hadn't fallen sullen or lost her temper. She hadn't managed to annoy Sophie or make her angry. Would she be angry now if she told her she was keeping things from Flora, the one person who had shown her nothing but kindness? From the person who had, in fact, brought Sophie into her life? But she couldn't lie now.

"No. I didn't tell anyone. Just you." It felt too intimate and she had to look away, embarrassment creeping across her skin.

"Then we have a secret?"

Mary kicked a rock with the toe of her shoe. "We do."

A sudden sharp clap startled her, and Mary looked up. Once again, Sophie was doing a kind of dance, this time, clapping her hands and moving her feet in quick little shuffles that made dust out of the dirt that lifted to her knees. "A secret! We have a real live secret!"

"Maybe we should see if it fits before we celebrate," Mary suggested, and the two girls approached the gate, their hearts thumping in their chests.

They pulled aside some vines and a few thorny rose branches that had grown over the top of the wall, revealing a small door. Near the handle was a small keyhole. Sophie bent down and peered through it.

"Non," she said, shaking her head as she stood straight. "You can't see nothing. Must be grown over. Try the key now."

Mary swallowed hard, her hand shaking the tiniest bit as she lifted the key and fit it into the hole, her mind racing with possibility.

*What if it doesn't turn? What if this isn't the key? What if the lock is rusted shut? What if . . . ?*

It turned, there was a small *click*, and the gate was unlocked before them.

The girls looked at each other first, then Mary extended her arm and pushed the gate inward. She caught her breath.

"Saint tonne le vie. Now this," Sophie said, a huge smile spreading over her beautiful face. "*This* is wild."

At one time, this may have been a well-curated garden. But now it was fingers of green grasping at every surface, threatening to tear down the walls that penned them in. It was now the beginning of June, and little brown was left except for here and there, where the overgrowth had stifled what was struggling underneath. A squat willow grew from the center, its long, flowing branches curled in the fists of rose and dogwood bushes; it bowed low like a child with her hair being yanked by younger siblings.

Mary stood by the door, the gate having only opened halfway for the roil of plant and shrubbery blocking its path, but Sophie waded in.

"This is like a bowl of soup," she declared. Her crow was back, and it cawed from its perch on the top ledge of the western wall as if in agreement. "It's like chowder. Like dumplings in bone broth!" She had to step careful and high, and sunk to her knees in some spots.

Mary was nervous even just watching her. "Careful! There's thorns in there."

Sophie turned and smiled. "Trousers are a girl's best friend, chére."

Mary looked down at her own bare legs, already scraped up from clambering over the Old Fort, and stayed where she was.

"There are sage bushes in here!" Sophie was excited, ducking now and then like a swimmer pulling below the surface and coming up for air. "And over there"—she pointed to the eastern barrier—"there's a line of cedar. Who knows what else is here. Things from other places, to be sure."

The air was different in here—thick and fragrant. It was the smell of good soil and the hard wood of creaking roots. There was the solid scent of fern and bush, and underneath, the soft aroma of wildflowers already in bloom—many shades of purple and a yellow hue for emphasis. Even with her untrained nose, Mary could make out cooking smells—dill and rosemary. It seemed like everything green in the whole earth was here, everything that could be eaten or steeped, ground up or used for infusing. It was as if the Georgian Bay had designated this spot of all the spots to be its apothecary, and now, it was theirs.

"Sophie?"

The taller girl popped up over by the cedar, a bright sprig of lavender tucked into her hat. "Yeah?"

"I think I might want to stay here after all."

---

The rest of the afternoon was passed in excited exploration. After a while and with Sophie's protestations that the thorns were all out in the open and could be avoided, Mary ventured in. It was strange to have so much greenery brushing against her skin, and at first, she recoiled from it.

"Can't be skittish in here." Sophie laughed, now chewing sweet clover while sitting on a natural ledge made by an elm branch that had scooped itself inside from beyond the garden's walls. "There's too much everywhere. No getting around it. Just go right into it, I say. Embrace it!"

Her enthusiasm was infectious, and maybe so was her courage, because before long, Mary was working to untangle the fronds of the willow so that the tendrils could move freely once more.

"We'll need gloves for most of this. There's too many prickly bits."

"Or we could grow thick skin," Sophie suggested, handing the last of her clover to the crow and swinging her legs off the branch before jumping down. "Callouses. They are like nature's glove."

"Yuck!" Mary twisted up her face. "I want gloves you can take off."

"But why?" Sophie joined her at the willow, unbraiding a creeping vine, careful not to sever its stalk. "Take them off for finery?" Then she grew serious, suddenly interested in the thought. "What fine things do you do in the manor, anyway?"

Mary was genuinely confused. "What do you mean . . . fine things?"

"Well, back in the settlement, we have balls. Not fancy ones, but good ones all the same. And we cook together and we play. No one stops us from running unless it's underfoot. And we sing loads. Do you have the grand balls, the ones with gowns? I saw a gown once."

Sophie talked like this often—long and wide without much room left for breathing. Mary didn't mind. She was slower to give up words and thoughts, and the other girl's whirlwind of conversation afforded her time to think.

"The manor is lonely," she finally answered. "It's a house without a heart, I think. Back in Toronto, we had fancy dinner parties, and the ladies wore hats. My parents went to dances and dinners outside, but I wasn't invited."

"Why not? You couldn't dance, you?"

Mary laughed. "No, because I'm a child. Children don't go to those things."

"Why not?"

Mary considered this and gave the answer she had heard

from her mother: "Because children do not attend the affairs of adults. It's not their place."

Sophie was silent for a moment, then remarked, "I think children's place is every place. Otherwise, why have 'em? Sounds boring to have a party with no kids around."

"When I have children," Mary said, "I plan on having them with me at all times. Except maybe at night. At night they can go with their nanny."

"Nanny? What in hell's a nanny?"

The hours went like this—exploring in the tangles, working to tame the larger green catastrophes of growth, and talking about everything in the entirety of existence. They didn't stop until the sun began to fall back from its peak.

"I have to get going. I'm butchering some rabbits for dinner, and home is a ways away," Sophie finally said, swiping at the sweat on her cheek and leaving a long streak of dirt in its place.

"A ways away," Mary repeated. "I like that. Your route home sounds like a poem."

"Do you know many poems?" Sophie sounded excited and suddenly Mary wished that she did. Sure, she had read many, but she had found them too frivolous to commit to memory. Now she regretted the dismissal. Anything that made Sophie animate like this was something she wanted to know.

"I'll find some," she said. "My uncle has books in his office. I'll find the ones with poems."

They were careful to lock up the gate after themselves and move the vines and branches back the way they had found them, before the wall had been breached. Then, somewhat reluctantly, the two friends made their way up the path toward the manor.

Even though she was exhausted, and even though her stomach grumbled over missed meals, Mary hoped it would take them forever to reach the back door.

# 11

# Into the Sky

Mary used to only ever be around flowers that were already taking that wilting march toward the garbage bin. Her mother would have impressive floral arrangements made up and delivered for events, beautiful creations of irises and lilies that made interesting silhouettes and showcased her mother's good taste—and good financial status to be able to commission them. Mary would watch these creations over the days they spent in the house, always thinking that the purpose of beauty was to die, to be cut and collected and curated and then die. She wondered if the blooms on taller stems would live longer since they had more height, as if death were seeping up the stalks and stems like poison. Her mother, on the other hand, would lose interest in them the day after the party and did not abide anything less than perfect.

*One dropped petal, and I want them gone*, she'd instruct the staff. *I don't need garbage on my tables, no matter how much it cost.*

Once, Mary had grabbed a handful of roses in an attempt to steal them away to her room so that they might stay a bit longer, and so that she might have something special and beautiful in her own room. This was how she learned the truth about roses: that they were covered in sharp thorns and dangerous to touch. That day, after running her palm under cool water to soothe the sting of a half dozen punctures, she'd carried that bouquet to the bin and dumped it in herself, vase and all. Beauty, she had decided, was nothing but superficial posturing and deep hurt. Beauty was not worth coveting since it would only cause you pain in the end.

But now, here she was, awake early and rummaging in her uncle's office looking for books that might betray any secrets about horticulture, and also looking for the poetry she had promised Sophie. She'd found a dusty volume with a convoluted title, *The Fundamentals of Horticulture and Landscape Suitability of the Northern Climes*. She already had the slim volume of *Romeo and Juliet* in the drawer of her desk from the night she and Olive had decided to put on their own two-man production. She figured it was a good enough book to stand in for Sophie's request of poetry.

In the week since Aunt Rebecca had come home, the woman had been making sure her presence was felt. For her part, Mary had been avoiding her, but Rebecca seemed to be everywhere. Mary had only been able to make it to the attic twice since she'd returned home, and on both occasions the door was locked. But she was able to slip a letter in through the bottom crack. Each time, she waited as long as she could, ear pressed to the door, waiting for some kind of movement from the other side that would indicate Olive had retrieved the missive. However there was nothing but the wind caught up in a soft shuffle along the floorboards whistling back.

Other than her disappointment over not seeing Olive, Mary's life had become quite amazing. Sophie came by nearly every day, and together they would head to their garden. They had quietly pocketed some of Jean's supplies—a pair of gloves, a small spade, an old hoe that had rusted and been left in the tall grass outside the cellar door. If Jean was outside already, Mary distracted him with questions about the difference between fennel and coriander, loamy soil from peat, while Sophie grabbed what they needed.

Flora no longer had to wake her; Mary was up, dressed, and out the door before the sun had fully risen. And on the third day of this routine, she woke to find a pair of tweed trousers draped over her desk chair. Mary was so overjoyed, she had to bite her lip to keep from giggling the whole time she put them on. Flora had guessed at measurements, but she'd done a remarkable job. When Mary mentioned it to her later, she replied, "'S nothing. When you have a whole bateau load of kids at home, you learn to size hand-me-downs." Mary ran and jumped and even climbed a tree that day while Sophie applauded, a captive audience.

The garden itself had changed as much as the girl. They'd used hedge clippers to tame the long grasses and found a flagstone path that led from the door to the willow. They'd worked all one afternoon to trim the greenery so that the stepping stones stood out, then jumped across them like frogs over a pond's surface. They'd used twine to wrangle the larger rosebushes that crawled instead of climbed, and pared the shrubs back into rounded scoops along the western wall.

That morning, Mary packed up the books she had taken from her uncle's shelves and carried them out the back in a picnic basket. She didn't run since there were also snacks in the basket, but she did walk as quickly as she could, over the yard, waving good morning to Jean who had just opened the first garden and was about to go in to prune the hedges.

"Morning, Jean," she called. "It's going to be a nice one, today."

The old man raised a hand to greet her back. He shook his head slow while she passed, skipping into the trees. That one was sure different, now, he thought. The Bay could do that if you let it. Then he returned to work, wondering where he had left his smaller clippers.

Sophie was already in the garden when Mary arrived. The door was closed and the air was quiet, but Mary knew. It might have been the little crow that followed her friend around, who now sat perched in the top corner where the walls met. Or it could have been the feeling she had on her skin that she was close by.

She wondered if other people felt this—the knowing feeling when someone you cared for was close. She'd heard people talk about it in reference to their children, but never about just a friend. She felt it like a shawl, but not one made of wool, not something heavy. It was more like silk. It was less comfort and more luxury, something slick and beautiful draped about her shoulders. But that wasn't it either, not really. This was like nothing she'd ever experienced before, and every now and then she'd gasp from the soft weight of it. Sometimes she even grew angry, thinking about it being taken away. In her experience, things didn't often stay, certainly not things of importance.

She hadn't even gotten in the door when Sophie called out, "Eh, lookit! Look what I've found!"

Wearing her customary slacks but stripped of her button-down men's shirt and wearing a thin undershirt that had seen better days (and bigger bodies), Sophie was under the willow, the weeds they had yet to tame up to her knees. She held up a board in her hands, presenting it to Mary as if it were a scepter of some importance.

"Wood?" There was something distracting about the girl, but even so, Mary couldn't see why she was smiling so big over a random plank.

"A swing!" She laughed, deep and somehow still childish in tone. It was a sound that bounced around under Mary's ribs like a caught echo. "Come, see. There's rope and iron hooks on the sides, and the wood's even formed to someone's derriere!"

"A swing?" Mary was walking forward, but she didn't hear Sophie anymore. Instead she heard another voice, one she had heard once in her backyard saying horrible things about her into the bright afternoon. *My mother wouldn't be pleased. Wasting time like this.*

"Mary, can you believe it? A swing. There must have been a child here once. Maybe Hattie's daughter, Olive."

Mary caught her breath. She hadn't even considered that Olive was a child that could have existed outside of the manor house. Now she was sad she had never asked her about it when they were still able to have visits. Ever since she had found the garden, there hadn't been one word shared between them, and every letter had gone unanswered.

"Did you know Olive?" Mary was greedy for details, the swing itself momentarily forgotten.

"Non, I was just young then, back when she took ill and never came back out. I ask Flora about her from time to time, but there's never much to say about that one." Sophie's voice was sad, like she couldn't imagine anything worse than being doomed to live a life on the inside of walls. "I think though, one day, maybe she'll come out again."

"Yes," Mary agreed, reaching out to touch the bleached wood in Sophie's hands. "Maybe if we get this garden in shape, maybe if we put her swing back, then she will come out."

"Maybe." Sophie shrugged. "Let's keep going, then. But you know, we'll need to make more once we have this one hung."

She shimmied up the tree, reaching the thickest branch and shaking it to test for strength. "Here, this will do. Looks like this is where it was, anyway." She pointed midway out and, sure enough, there were two indents worn smooth into the bark where a rope might have carried weight.

Mary shaded her eyes with her hand, looking up through the cascading tendrils to watch Sophie's strong arms, bare in the sun, grip and flex to hold her in the tree. "You mean it? We can make more?"

Sophie smiled down at her. "Sure, I can do it. Did you bring something to read to me while I work?"

Mary thought there couldn't be a more perfect feeling in the world than the one she had right now. Except that she was just beginning to understand that there were so many new ways for her to feel, both very good and very bad, and they were about to arrive in the secret garden.

---

At dinner, she drank her milk without wincing. There was an art to pleasing Aunt Rebecca. It wasn't exactly elegant and there was no way to practice for it, but it was a job nonetheless. It involved maintaining composure and making expressions small and polite. One had to agree without opinion, move without sound, and be present but not take up too much space. Lucky for Mary, these were all skills she had honed while under her mother's roof.

Only Rebecca was shrewder than Cecile ever was. It probably had to do with their polar opposite social schedules. Where Cecile had been distracted, busy to a fault, and sleepy when stuck inside the house without company, Rebecca was bored, and she resented this boredom. It made her angry, and she liked to project her anger. So, whereas her mother could go a whole day without noticing Mary, Rebecca made it a point to seek her out, to examine and judge until there was something to complain about.

Such as when Mary entered the dining room one day after carefully cleaning the dirt and smell of the outside off every inch of her body, changing into one of the dresses Rebecca preferred—one not too flashy as to remind her of her own station, but not too shabby as to make her feel ashamed.

"Have you always walked like that?"

"Like what, Aunt Rebecca?"

"Like a cat," Rebecca sniffed. She hated all animals. "Like a smug, self-absorbed cat."

There was no way to respond to this that could be considered a win. If Mary asked her how she should walk instead, then she would be accused of insolence, of talking back, of being dense on purpose. But if she didn't adjust her offending walk, then she was being disobedient, of tormenting her charitable aunt with behavior she already knew bothered her. From trial and error on other criticisms—like the way she "wore her hair like a tavern girl" or the way she "chewed like a savage"—Mary knew it was best to ask Rebecca for a demonstration of the proper way to do things. Rebecca liked to think of herself as a role model. Ironically, she was very smug about it, self-absorbed, even.

So on the day Sophie had found and hung the old swing and began fashioning the start of the second one, the day Mary read to a beautiful girl under the awning of a weeping willow, she did everything she could to keep her aunt happy. She didn't want anything pulling her out of her mood. She couldn't bear the thought of having to fill her head with different images. Everything was perfect just as it was.

Her happiness was something that, as it turned out, was another thing that grated on the woman of the house.

"A child without a serious task is a foolish child," she began, taking an audible sip of her tea. "And I can see by the foolish look on your face today that you are in need of something serious."

"Oh no, Aunt. I am taking my outdoor education very seriously. In fact, I was hoping to spend more time in the gardens."

Rebecca sneered. "More time? We barely see you as it is."

Flora, who had come quietly into the dining room carrying a fresh pot of tea, gave Mary a side glance. She knew Sophie had been over every chance she had, even though the mistress of the house did not.

"No," Rebecca continued. "It's time to consider your education. Not that you need to learn a trade or worry about college like a young man. But you do need to know the things that will make you a good wife."

Mary worked very hard not to roll her eyes.

"Starting next week, Thomas March will be coming over to teach you proper French, not like the pigeon patois the half-breeds around here call French. Thomas was trained in Montreal, so he will teach you the real language."

Mary slammed her milk glass a little too hard on the table. "Why?"

Rebecca took a beat before answering, keeping her eyes on

her plate. "For one thing, it's obvious you need to be interacting with more educated and cultured people."

Flora gave a small cough on her way back out of the room, as if alerting the table that she was still within earshot. If Rebecca heard her, she didn't let on.

"It's like the saying—those who lie down with dogs get up with fleas."

"Hold on—"

"And I will not have dogs in my house. So in three days, Mr. March will be here after breakfast, and you will begin lessons. There will not be a discussion about it."

Mary sighed, threw herself back in her chair, and folded her arms over her chest. "How long will he be here?"

"He will have lunch with us, as lessons will end mid-afternoon." Rebecca dabbed the corner of her mouth with her napkin and tossed it on the table. "And you will be on your best behavior. Because if you can't do lessons in the house, then you'll do them at a boarding school, is that clear?"

The idea of being sent away leapt into Mary's throat and made words impossible. She couldn't leave, would not leave—not Olive or Sophie or even Flora and Jean and Philomene. And there was no way she could walk away from the secret garden now. She had finally found a place where she fully belonged, and she had carved it out of the wilds herself—well, with some help from Sophie . . . a lot of help. But now she would have to spend hours every day inside, with some stranger, learning a language she didn't care for. Hours when she could be pruning, or laughing, or even swinging into the sky.

"I wish you had never come back."

She said it low but firm and regretted it as soon as the words were out of her mouth. This was a woman who could make her life miserable, who had *already* made her life miserable. But it was the truth, so she tilted her chin up and held her shoulders back.

Rebecca winced, a small, defensive movement. Her cheeks flushed for a moment before she collected herself, pushed back her chair with a screech, and stood to her full height. She put both hands carefully on the table and leaned in toward the girl. "And I wish you had never shown up. There wasn't exactly a line of people willing to take you."

Now it was Mary's turn to flush. She could hear her blood in her veins, feel every inch of her exposed skin. She sat there, stewing in her fury, until Rebecca, satisfied she had hit her target, turned and sashayed out of the room. Then Mary stood and bolted from the dining room, through the kitchen—not stopping to answer Flora calling after her—and ran all the way to the garden.

The air was still warm, but the sun had already started its slow summer descent, so the light was more solid and less real at the same time. There was no glare, no white heat. Everything was shadows and outlines. The walls, where the vines pulled away into tangle, were very gray, and the willow leaves were the shape and color of new snap peas. Already, the apple tree that grew in the back corner was beginning to flower—white blooms cheerful against the backdrop of deep pines looming over the wall.

With tears in her eyes and a sob caught in her chest, Mary stepped carefully over the flagstones they'd unearthed. Even now, it made her think of a frog hopping on waxy lily pads. But now there was no joy in it; there was only the sense of loss—the loss of what had already been taken, and the overwhelming loss of what could still be snatched away. Crickets strummed soft music in the weeds, a tiny symphony for her brokenness.

She wished she was still angry, wished that she could pin all this darkness that collected and rumbled in her bones on her aunt. She wanted to believe that the words spoken were untrue, were wrathful, were vindictive. And for sure, they could have been. But Mary knew deep down that they were also true. Who would have wanted her? Who could have a soft spot for a girl like her?

She made her way under the skirts of the willow and sat on the swing Sophie had carefully rehung. It creaked under her slight weight but held steady. The branches arching overhead showed the silver from underneath and made a soft rustle as she settled onto the wooden seat. Only now did it occur to her that maybe this was not a good place for a swing.

They'd been so excited to finish it, they'd attached it to the branch without much thought. But now it hung in shadows beside the craggy trunk and hemmed in by the elegant weep of the low tendrils.

"Of course," Mary scoffed. "How appropriate."

She dug the toes of her shoes into the dirt and set herself into a bit of a small spin.

Mary knew she was not what some people might call "an easy child." Even when she was very young, she didn't laugh or run or do the adorable things that other toddlers did. There were no sweet songs, no sticky-handed hugs, no running or dancing with any sort of wild abandon. She had always been observant, watching, listening. These were traits that made grown-ups uneasy coming from a small child.

A woman had once even approached Miss Patricks about it. *Is there something the matter with that child? She's just . . . staring.* Mary remembered Miss Patricks answering with a shrug. She, like the woman, took that shrug to mean that Mary did indeed have "something the matter" with her and that also there was nothing that could be done about it.

In Toronto, there were often people at her house, but none that belonged to her, none that came specifically for her or stayed for her or even really noticed her. She didn't make friends in her classes or at church, and people generally avoided making conversation when they could. She considered now that perhaps this is why she had become so close to

Olive in such a short amount of time. Both girls knew what it was to be locked away from the world. Both understood the movement of the world when it is only observed and never engaged.

In the dark shadows of the tree, there was a sudden movement on the ground that caught Mary's eye and pulled her back into the moment. It was a slice in the tall grass of some weight pulling the blades to bend, and it was inching toward her. She watched as it paused, then continued forward.

Finally, a small head poked through. A snake! It stuck its tongue out, a flicking pink ribbon, sniffing the air in her direction.

Mary squealed and lifted her feet off the ground. "Go away!" she shouted, dipping a foot to kick some dirt toward it. This motion set the swing rocking. "Get!"

She kicked again and the swing moved more. The snake, however, did not move. It lay there in the grass, its head bobbing slightly to follow her motion. She kicked at the air, forcing the swing higher, farther away from the snake. And soon Mary was pumping hard, leaning back to catch more momentum. After a moment of air and flex and the wind rushing into her hair, she looked down, but the snake had disappeared. She kept swinging.

Soon her feet were touching the wall of willow branches that hung like a drape of lacy curtains—she had reached the end of her space. But instead of slowing down, Mary pumped harder, leaned farther back, her legs were breaking through the leaves up to her knees, then her waist, and then, finally, with one great push, her whole body broke through the arch and out on the other side.

She opened her eyes, which until then she hadn't realized were closed, and took a deep breath, the last contraction of the June sun bright on her face. It was like coming up from the bottom of the lake, like breathing for the first time. She didn't care that it took a snake to scare her into this discovery; she just enjoyed the feeling of resurfacing again and again. She understood that whoever had placed this swing here in the first place must have known this feeling, had maybe even chosen the spot for this reason—to be reborn again and again, on the momentum of your own muscle, into the sky.

Sometimes, even in the darkness, if you just push hard enough, you can end up sailing into the bright open.

# 12

# A Secret Visit Raises a Big Question

She had three days until Mr. March came to commence lessons, stealing away the plummiest hours from Sophie and the garden and the joy she had come to hold as the very center of her existence. Three days to store up enough of her freedom that she had memories to carry her through conjugating verbs and learning the nature of gendered nouns.

The first day, she cried while telling Sophie about the new interruption as they sat on rocks down at the shore. The girl listened to her tell her teary tale before doing what she did best—making everything better with a slight adjustment of perspective.

"So then, you come and teach me the proper Français after the man leaves, and I will teach you how to do this in return." She stood, took two steps, and turned a perfect cartwheel, her bare feet splashing into the water's edge. Mary giggled a bit, wiping at her eyes as Sophie took a deep bow. "It'll be School for Wilder Girls! And then, when we get to writing the words out, we'll do it here." Sophie grabbed a stick and drew the loopy letters of Mary's name in the wet sand.

"But we'll lose so much time," Mary lamented.

"Hey now." Sophie sat back down beside her. "You told me you weren't leaving, yeah? That means we have so much time. All the time. We can spend some of it learning."

They raced each other to the garden and finished crafting the second swing with a length of chain "borrowed" from Jean's shed. But before they could hang it, Mary was called in for supper, so they made a plan to meet up the next day.

"We should bring something to christen it," Mary suggested. "Like they do with ships."

"How do they do that, like with a priest pourin' water and that?"

She had to hold back her laughter since Sophie was quite serious in her query. "No, like with a bottle. You smash it over the prow before its maiden voyage."

"That's ridiculous. I'll never understand the British, me. Just bring our book. We'll read some pretty words before we take to the sky."

Sophie had become very attached to *Romeo and Juliet*, even though she thought Shakespeare was a "piss-poor storyteller" when it came down to it. She explained that the people in her community were known for stories, all sorts, and that this old man from across the ocean couldn't hold a candle to the weakest of them. But, being as she was empathetic and also at an age when everything was romantic in the wildest sense, the characters in the play became people Sophie cared deeply about and would not miss any opportunity to hear about them.

Mary, who had never been one for the bard herself (she preferred the women writers when it came to proper observation and finding the exact turns of phrase to capture them), she treasured the book for reasons she couldn't find words for, since she wasn't one of those writers she so admired. It was as if it had meaning under the story now. She read it aloud slowly during the day, to stretch out the tale, then reread the same passages at night, imagining that Romeo wore suspenders over a white shirt and was prone to turning flips through the cobbled streets of Italy.

The second day began as usual—early and hurried, with Mary dressing quickly and without any prodding. She made her way quietly down the stairs and composed herself before walking through the dining room doorway, making sure to straighten her posture and take on the glazed but focused look that seemed to work best when greeting Aunt Rebecca. But when she entered, she was greeted by a sight she hadn't seen in weeks—Flora and Philomene seated at the table. Flora was helping herself to a cup of tea.

"What are you doing here?" Mary blurted.

"Well, good morning to you, too," Flora responded, pausing mid-pour.

This was how things had been at the start: the staff wandering in and out of the house, Flora joining her for meals, and once in a while, Philomene popping in to listen to Flora talk about weather or old ways or the right way to deal with dandelions (brew them into tea, would be the correct answer). But it hadn't been like this in so many days, it threw Mary for a loop.

"Aren't you . . . ?" she began, then turned quick to look behind her and lowered her voice into a whisper. "Aren't you going to get in trouble from Rebecca?"

Flora's eyes got big and her mouth opened into a round O. She feigned horror with her hands, open as wide as her eyes on either side of her face. "Dieu! You are right! What will we do? Philomene, we need to hide!"

The old woman, who couldn't hold the charade, laughed.

"All right, very funny." Mary didn't like being made fun of, and that's clearly what this was.

"Oh child. Sit. Eat. Look, we made eggs and bacon and brought out three kinds of preserves. No nutrition regime this morning." Flora plopped two cubes of sugar into her cup as punctuation to the statement.

Mary sunk into a seat beside Philomene, who pushed a platter of flapjacks closer to her. "But where is she?"

"Gone," Flora sang. "Once a month for a full day, from sunrise to late past sunset, we get our own miracle when Madame heads to her cousin's house on the other side of the Bay. I only wish she'd stay longer . . ."

"Every month?" Mary forked two pancakes onto her plate and poured generously from the syrup jug. She was smiling, but then her shoulders drooped a little. "Only *once* a month?"

The three paused and then laughed together as one. It was the best breakfast she'd had in weeks. She hadn't realized how much she missed this food until she was on her second helping, piling thick bacon to soak up the pool of syrup left from the first course.

"Sooooo, I hear you have a gentleman coming over to spend time with you," Flora sang.

"What? I do not," Mary answered honestly.

"Mr. March?"

Philomene cocked her head. "Qui?"

"Little Thomas March, that English boy whose father owns the new boat shop in town?" Flora explained, and Philomene nodded. "But who would get an English to build their boat for this Bay, I don't know. Anyway, Madame hired him to teach our Mary."

"Oh yes, the tutor," Mary scoffed. Despite Sophie's enthusiasm for their "shared lesson," she was still not looking forward to her schooling. "I told her I didn't need anyone to teach me French. I'm busy enough as it is."

"Miss Mary, Rebecca is hoping you learn more than just a li'l language. She is setting you up."

Mary didn't look up from the toast she was buttering. "Setting me up for what?"

"Mon dieu." Flora rolled her eyes. "You are fifteen now. And proper ladies start looking to match up." When Mary reached for the jam, unfazed, it was clear she still had no idea what was going on. "For marriage, you petite chou."

Mary dropped the knife. "*Marriage?*"

"Oui." Philomene chuckled. "I was married at thirteen, me."

"Then you're already late," Flora added, and the two women laughed.

"This isn't funny!" Mary's chair scraped across the floor and she stood abruptly. "I am a child! Much too young to begin considering . . . I mean, who would do such a thing? What a trick! I won't have it! Is he . . . is he coming to marry me next week? Oh God, am I being forced into a wedding with a stranger?"

"Cherie, your mother never talked to you about how all this business goes?" Flora spoke gentler now—clearly she hadn't expected a girl of fifteen to still be so naive.

"She didn't really talk . . . to me." Mary nearly fell back into her chair. Flora poured her a cup of tea, and Philomene passed it down to the distraught girl, patting her hand and placing it on the saucer.

"Well, Mr. Thomas, he will come over, probably with books, and probably all washed up and smelling sweet. He will teach you whatever nonsense he is supposed to teach, but all the while it will be a kind of test," Flora explained.

"A French test?" Mary took a sip of the hot tea.

"Non, non. A love test, kind of. You'll spend time together, under your patron's roof so it's proper. Someone will always be close by, see. And then you and the boy, you talk. And you see how you like each other. And if you do? Then well . . . you marry. But much later."

Flora did her best to sell it. There were some things in life that were inevitable for girls like Mary—wealthy girls, white girls. For the most part, they were brought into marriages like livestock, the decisions heavily influenced by their families. The Marches and the Cravens were both from British bloodlines, and both were very wealthy, even by city standards.

"Can I say no?" Mary had regained some of her composure now that she knew she wasn't going to be wearing a white gown to her first tutoring session.

"Of course," Flora said. "No one wants a miserable wife. Times are changed from that. But still, if the families want it, they will push hard. You'll see."

"But what if I don't like him like that?" Mary's voice

was small. Her stomach felt all twisted up. She had the urge to run.

"Well then, you just push back," Flora said, nodding her head once, her lips tight. "You be strong and you push."

"And . . . what if . . . I already like someone else like that?" Now there was color in her cheeks. Mary didn't know she was going to ask it before it came out of her mouth, but there it was, on the breakfast table along with the dirty dishes and the jars of jam.

Philomene and Flora exchanged a quick glance. "Well then, cherie," Flora said carefully, "you have to decide how much you can push until someone starts pushing back. That's how you start a brawl."

Suddenly Mary was full to burst, and she was worried she might vomit all over Aunt Rebecca's good linen. "May I be excused?"

"Of course," Flora answered.

Mary stood up and walked slowly out of the room, as if she were sleepwalking. Her mind was somewhere else, somewhere confused and scared. She would go to her room for a bit and lie down.

Just as she reached the door, Flora spoke, her voice louder and pitched higher than normal. "Uh, I just want you to know, there, I may not be around later on if you're looking for me. I have to take on extra duties as well as Madame's errands while she is gone. That means rearranging the pantry, hanging the laundry, going up to the third floor, dusting the buffet . . ." She paused, shaking her head and pursing her lips. "Hmm. Sometimes though, I am so forgetful. I hope I remember to lock everything back up when I'm done. Would be a shame . . ."

Mary was so preoccupied over this whole courting business she almost let Flora's obvious message pass right over her head. But then she understood. She turned on a heel, breath held. Suddenly she didn't want to go to her room. "Really?"

"One can never be sure 'bout these things," Flora answered, one eyebrow raised.

Mary was about to launch into a full run, but she took a moment and composed herself. "Merci, Flora. Merci, Philomene. For the breakfast. And for the truth."

And then she took off through the kitchen and out the back door before life could catch up to her again.

---

"Do you think she's left yet?"

"Shhhh!"

Mary and Sophie were crouched outside the kitchen door, waiting and listening, the garden all but forgotten for the day. They hadn't even gotten around to hanging their second swing. But now Sophie was already bored and had begun picking clovers and braiding their long stems together. She was like a small child that way, Mary thought. Always needing to be entertained or she drifted off in thought and began to fidget.

"It's gotta be past lunch now."

"Patience!" Mary hissed. "We can't just waltz up there if Flora is still there. That would put her in an awkward situation. This way she can honestly say she forgot to lock the door if we get caught."

"But the mean one, your aunt, she's gone from the house, yes?"

"Yes, but you never know. The devil has an awful way of finding things out."

Sophie laughed. "You have some funny ways of talking, especially about ole Lucifer."

Then they heard Flora's voice in the kitchen. She was speaking French to Philomene.

"Okay," Sophie whispered. "She's telling Philly lunch was served and that they should go out on the front porch and sweep up."

The girls waited until the women's footsteps grew faint, then stood and snuck into the kitchen. Sophie grabbed a dinner roll from the counter as they passed, shoving it in her mouth whole. They moved quick and low, both to avoid attracting attention and also because it was more fun to imagine that they were on a true covert mission and not one that had been prearranged.

“Hurry, and hold the rails, the steps are uneven,” Mary whispered.

“I know how to walk, me,” Sophie shot back. Then she stumbled, the piece of bread in her mouth flying out.

Mary glared, waited until the taller girl pocketed the projectile, stood, and firmly grasped the railing. Then they made their way onto the second floor.

“Mon dieu, this place is huge,” Sophie marveled, looking up and down the long hallway. “Which is yours?”

Mary felt a sudden shyness, but she pointed toward her door, which is where Sophie went. They didn’t have time for this. They should go straight to the attic. She wanted to say this out loud, but she couldn’t find her voice. Instead, she held her right elbow with her left hand, bit the inside of her cheek, and followed.

“Wow.” Sophie walked into the room and turned in a slow circle, taking it all in. Mary stayed in the doorframe. The space seemed so much smaller with Sophie in it. She was tall and she was wild and she was the biggest thing in Mary’s life. It was almost impossible that she could exist in this room, within these four unremarkable walls. She thought about how many hours she’d spent in here thinking about Sophie, and now here she was, in real life.

Just last night she had thought about the two of them in the abandoned house, the one they had gone to on that first day. Only in her daydream, they had fixed it up the same way they had fixed up the garden. There was a table with a lacy cloth and four wooden chairs. There were cupboards and an icebox and even a braided rug on the ground. The sconces on the walls held candles, and they had picked a bouquet of garden roses for the centerpiece. It made her feel less alone in her bed, in her room, in this house where she didn't quite belong.

"Don't you get lonely?" Sophie asked.

"What?"

"In a room all by yourself? I've never had a whole room just for me," she said, standing over the little writing desk and looking out the back window. "What do you do in here?"

Mary blushed. "We should go."

"Lead the way," Sophie answered, placing her forearm across her stomach and bowing deeply, sweeping her arm out as she straightened up, just like an old-timey gentleman.

---

Mary held her breath at the top of the stairs with her hand on the knob. She paused, blowing all the air out of her lungs. This was it. Behind her in the darkened stairwell, Sophie leaned her body against Mary's back.

"You gonna try it or what?"

"Yeah, yeah." Mary tried not to notice the way Sophie's weight was affecting her, how she wanted to stand right here, just like this, for just a moment longer. And then she tried the knob. And, unlike the last few weeks, it turned.

They let the door swing open all the way before stepping up onto the floorboards.

"Olive?" Mary whispered. "You awake?"

The air felt stale. It had gotten hot outside, and while it was cooler up here than in the rest of the house, it was also somehow less.

"Olive?"

When Mary had last been up here, after a week of dancing and giggling into pillows and even hanging some of the stored art so that the walls had more cheer, it had been a place that was beginning to resemble a bedroom rather than a sickroom. But the attic she and Sophie entered now had been bleached of all that cheer. It felt like the space had been stripped of color and mood, and it was all sepia and flat.

"There's really a girl up here?" Sophie whispered now, not because they needed to stay quiet, but because one whispers in places like churches and funeral parlors.

"There is," Mary answered before calling out again in a louder whisper, "Olive!"

The bed curtains were all pulled closed, and suddenly, Mary was scared. What if her cousin was dead? She dismissed the thought as quick as it came since Flora would have told her. But the air had this strange quality of lack that she had to say it aloud to remind herself. "She's not dead."

Sophie must have felt that emptiness, too, because she didn't question the statement. Instead, she gave a quick, solemn nod, and together, they moved to the foot of the bed. Mary grasped the edges of two curtains where they met and yanked them back all at once. And there, in the center of the huge bed, was her beloved cousin, Olive. Or rather, a small, pale version of her.

"Olive!" Mary scrambled onto the huge bed. "Oh, what happened? You look worse than ever!"

Olive roused at the movement and opened her eyes. They were swollen, and the whites were a dim yellow. "Mary," she croaked, and tried to smile. "I am so happy to see you."

"Mon dieu, she's in bad shape, her," Sophie finished with a whistle.

Mary shot her a sharp look, but Olive responded with a small laugh, a motion that made her press her palm against her chest. "I am in bad shape, the worst shape."

"I don't understand," Mary said. She placed the back of her hand against the girls' forehead. "No fever." Really, she had no idea what would constitute a fever, but when her nanny had done this for her as a child, it seemed a fever announced itself without any doubt. "You were so much better when I saw you last."

"Oh, those were fun days," Olive said, trying to pull herself up to sit.

"No, no, you stay lying," Mary cooed. "You really can't be

moving too much." She tried to sound calm, but there were alarm bells going off in her head. "What happened? Why are you so ill now?"

Olive shrugged her slender shoulders, and Mary thought there were tears in her eyes. "Since Rebecca—since my stepmother," she corrected herself, and Mary understood this was nonnegotiable with Rebecca. "Since she came home, things have gotten worse. I thought maybe it was just because I missed you so much."

Mary felt a pain around where she thought her heart must be. She had never noticed the physical location of that organ before coming to Craven Manor, and now she had begun to feel it in extremes—swinging one way and then the other, like breaking through branches and into the sky and then falling back down into the dirt. "I missed you, too. I wasn't allowed to see you. I tried . . ."

"I know. I got your letters." Olive smiled, her eyes closed against the sunlight Sophie had let in by opening a window. "I hid them, under the mattress."

She patted the bed beside her, near the edge, and continued. "But it's more than that, I think. I am dizzy all the time now. Worse than ever before you came."

Mary remembered her first visit. "Your medicine. You had stopped taking it, like I said?"

Olive nodded and Mary felt the icy fingers of panic start to wrap around her spine. "Oh my God, this is my fault. I told you to stop taking it and now you're dying! I mean, probably, I don't know!" She got off the bed and began pacing, her arms crossed over her chest, rubbing at the opposite arm in a feeble attempt to self-comfort.

"But I got better," Olive interrupted. "Remember? I was so much better."

"Yes, you were . . ."

"And we played and we even jumped." Olive smiled at the memory. "And I could stay awake long enough to read, and it didn't make me nauseous."

"What changed, then?" Mary stopped walking. Something occurred to her. "Did your doctor see how much better you were? What did he say?"

"He hasn't come. Only Rebecca." Olive had given up the pretense of stepmotherhood now. "Rebecca said it was a false sign, said my energy was a sign that the disease was taking a turn for the worse."

"What kind of bullshit is that?" Sophie interjected, her eyes narrowed. "I've never heard of such a thing."

"I drank less and less of the medicine like you said, and watered it down, but then she took the bottle away and came back with a new one." Olive pointed to the side table where a thick, dark green glass bottle stood.

Sophie held it up to the light, turning it this way and that so that the liquid sloshed about, the sediment on the bottom moving like a storm cloud behind the dark glass. "Your doctor gives you this?"

"No. He gives me those." Olive lifted her hand and pointed a shaking finger at the smaller glass container on her nightstand.

Mary picked that one up. There was a label affixed to the side, and written in loopy letters was a date and Olive's name. "Maybe these are what's making you sick, then?"

She unscrewed the metal top and shook a few pills into her palm. They were round and white. She jiggled her hand and one flipped over. She squinted to read the letters embedded in its smooth surface.

"This is just aspirin," she said, her tone betraying her surprise. "My mother used to take these every day. These are common."

Olive didn't respond, not understanding what Mary was getting at.

"If you are so sick"—she gestured to the prone figure on the bed—"as sick as all this, why are you only getting aspirin?"

Sophie had meanwhile popped the cork stopper out the neck of the bottle and was sniffing the contents. "Merde. This smells foul."

Mary was confused. How could her cousin be this bad off? She was jumping and playing and reciting Shakespeare the last time she was up here. "Olive, if the doctor gives you these pills, where does *that* come from?"

Olive looked up, her eyes fluttering to open and focus. "Rebecca."

Sophie leaned in again to smell the bottle. "This smells bad, cherie."

Mary shrugged. "Medicine always smells bad. Tastes worse."

"No, no. It smells like something is *wrong*," Sophie insisted. She put the bottle to her mouth and tipped it back so the liquid wet her lips. She touched her top lip with her tongue and winced. "Oh wah, there is something . . . a root?" She was talking to herself now. "Non, not a root. But not a plant either. What is that?"

She put the bottle down on the table and started walking around the room, her eyes darting here and there. She began opening every drawer on one of the random dressers along the back wall.

"What are you looking for?" Mary asked.

"A bowl, or something like that." Sophie cupped her hands together to show the shape she needed.

"For what?"

"Help look?"

They both searched until Sophie found a crystal flower vase in the back of a wardrobe. "La!"

Then she went back to the bed, picked up the murky bottle from the side table, and dumped its contents into the vase.

"What are you doing?" Mary asked. "Don't make a mess, or we'll all get in trouble."

"I need to see this," Sophie answered distractedly. "All this here."

She held the vase in both hands, walked over to the window where the light was best, and carefully lifted it above her head. She turned her head on an angle so she could look directly at the bottom of the clear glass.

"Ah!" she cried out. The sudden sound roused Olive to pull herself up on her pillows.

Mary walked over, crouching down so she could look at whatever had grabbed Sophie's attention. But all she saw was a layer of mushy silt. "What?"

"See that?" Sophie said.

"See what?"

"A kind of, like a . . ." She searched for the right word. "Maybe a confiture?"

"What's that?" Mary had her nose pressed almost on the glass now, but she still couldn't make anything out.

"Like, how do you say . . . ?"

"Jam," Olive said thinly. "Confiture is jam."

"Yes! Like how in jam there's bits of fruit skin and then the insides. They separate like this," Sophie explained.

"So Rebecca has been giving Olive . . . jam?" Mary asked with a bit of a laugh that had no mirth in it.

"Not that." Sophie was getting frustrated trying to explain. She lowered the vase and placed it on the ledge of the window. The sun shone through the cut crystal and sent colors onto the floor, as if it were the strange treasure at the end of a rainbow.

"There are berries in here," Sophie finally explained. "And me? I don't think they're the good kind neither. Might even be snakeberry."

"Snakeberry?"

"Oui. Some call it baneberry. Grows white or red—both poison though."

Mary paused a moment to take it all in. "Do you think it could be making her sick? Sicker than she really is?"

"The wrong berry can make you spend all your days in bed." Sophie stopped herself but then finished her thought. There was no room for holding back when it came to what could be found in the forest and what, in the wrong hands, those things could do. "All your days until your last one."

Mary gasped. "So, what do we do now? Should we say something to Rebecca?"

"Like what?"

"Like, 'you made a mistake and you're making Olive really sick'?!" Mary was getting frantic. "I mean, we'll get in trouble for sneaking up here. Flora, too. But we have to. We just have to tell her!"

Sophie locked eyes with Mary and lowered her voice so Olive couldn't overhear. "And what if it's no mistake? What then?"

Mary swallowed. As much as she wanted to rescue her cousin, like the prince who climbed Rapunzel's hair, she was out of ideas. "I don't know what to do."

Sophie took her hand and gave it a quick squeeze. "I do." She poured the contents back into the bottle and headed for the door.

---

"You think what?!" Flora's hand was held out, her mouth agape.

Mary and Sophie had held hands on the way down the stairs, out to the front to gather the women, and to the kitchen. Mary needed the support. She was not used to having allies in telling those in charge what was on her mind, and she might have changed her mind and bolted if not for Sophie's resolve. And now they all stood in the kitchen—Mary, Sophie, Flora, and Philomene—the green bottle of Rebecca's home remedy on the counter between them.

"We're not saying she knows exactly—it could be by accident," Mary said. She glanced furtively at Sophie, who had hoisted herself up onto the counter and was chewing on a toothpick, her eyes on the floor. She continued, still bumbling her way to the point, "There's no accusation, only a question about intent. But we couldn't say nothing. Not when Olive is getting sicker."

Flora placed her hands on her hips. "That girl has been sick since she was wee."

"Not the same way," Philomene chimed in. All eyes turned to her. "When she was small, her, she didn't like outside. She didn't like people. She cried, her. It was her fadder who decided then that she was sick. Me? I think she was just sad."

"Sad?" Mary echoed.

"Oui, a sad child. In her head, maybe her heart, too. But when Madame showed up, well, you can only martyr yourself for a sick child if the child is physically sick. Craven couldn't say no then. Not to a saint." She smacked her lips, a deeper sound than a regular *tsk*. "That's when the girl, she got sick like this, now."

There was a full minute of silence while they all took this in.

"We have no proof," Flora finally said. "We can't really say anything."

"Flo," Sophie said. "We can't leave it. The girl, have you seen her?"

"I have." Flora sighed, sitting on a tall kitchen stool, then springing back up right away, restless with worry. "And I know. All I'm saying is we can't say anything, not yet. But we have to do something."

"We need to talk to my uncle," Mary offered. "I can write him."

"We need to do something before that," Flora replied. "A letter takes days from up here, maybe a week or more to get to him. And even then, what do we say?" She repeated Mary's earlier comment, not unkindly. "We don't have an accusation, only a question."

Sophie leapt down from the counter. "I know! I have a solution for right now. Not for forever, but it's something we can do right now. Flora? How long does one of these bottles last before she makes a new one?"

"I don't know, about a week? Maybe ten days?"

"And she makes sure it's being taken, yeah?"

Flora nodded.

Sophie clapped her hands together, the toothpick still in the corner of her mouth. "Then we make a new batch ourselves. It'll look the same, almost smell the same, and then we have ten days to figure out something else. But that's ten days Olive won't be getting sicker, if we're right."

"Can we do that?" Mary quickly asked, hopeful for the first time since they'd ventured into Olive's sickroom. "Is it possible?"

"Oh cherie," Sophie said. "It is possible. Between the three of us—" she nodded to her kin in the room and then, in an act of charity, included Mary. "I mean, with your help of course, we can conjure up something real good. Might even help the poor kid."

They poured the mixture into a bowl, took turns examining and sniffing, and began to gather the ingredients they would need for an identical placebo. This involved Mary being sent out into the back to gather random plants. Jean came in handy with that. She didn't know what plantain might look like, or rat root, so his expertise was needed. Since the gardener wasn't one for asking questions or getting involved in other people's business, it was quick work. And a full hour before Rebecca Craven was due to return home, the little team had delivered the same bottle with a very different sort of medicine back to the attic and their patient.

"Now listen close, love," Flora explained to Olive, sitting on the edge of the bed. "You are going to take your medicine as usual, yeah? The same way you always do. If you complain, then keep complaining. If you take it with a sour face, then make that sour face. Everything the same. But just know, there's nothing in there that will hurt you anymore."

Olive was confused and sweaty with the fever Mary had failed to detect. "What's wrong with the medicine?" she whispered. "Mary said it might be making me sicker?"

"We don't know, us. Not for sure. We're just . . . being extra careful." Flora wiped the girl's face with the hem of her apron. "We're just seeing if this helps. But here's the next big thing, listen careful. If you do start to feel better, like before, don't let on."

Olive's brow furrowed. "Why not?"

"Just take my word for it, eh? Just stay in bed, stay lying down until you're all alone for sure. And don't get caught. Just stay in bed as much as you can. I'll find a way to come check on you. But you only tell me if you're feeling better."

Olive nodded. "But what if I don't feel better?"

Flora exhaled loudly and looked directly at Mary and Sophie when she answered. "Then we will have the answer to our question. Once and for all."

# 13

# Mr. Thomas March at the Manor

Now they had a secret. A big one. Bigger than the garden, even.

Mary went to bed early that night, afraid that if she saw Rebecca, the woman would immediately know about everything—the attic trip, the new medicine, the plan, all of it—just by looking at her.

She was relieved when her aunt was too tired from her journey to attend breakfast with the rest of them the next morning. And when she appeared at a quarter to ten, she was too distracted with last-minute instructions to pay any attention to Mary. If she had, she had mistaken Mary's nerves over the whole clandestine affair to be nerves about the start of her lessons.

"Flora, go give her hair a good brushing and splash some rose water on her," Rebecca said, circling Mary like a drill sergeant at inspection. "And Mary? Whenever you feel like saying something, think twice and say half."

Mary had forgotten about the fact that her tutor was really a suitor in disguise until just now. But instead of filling with anxiety, she was filled with relief. What was a boy in the face of all this new Olive drama? She gladly went with Flora for her last-minute preparations.

Mr. Thomas March showed up at ten o'clock on the dot. He carried a leather briefcase, wore small spectacles and a grand hat, and appeared with all the seriousness and pomp of a small man attending an important meeting. And this was how he presented himself to Flora when she opened the door.

Seeing Flora there, he snatched his glasses off his face and jammed them in his suit jacket pocket. "Good morning, I am here on the behest of Mrs. Craven. Might she or Mary Craven be available?"

"Thomas March, you are all grown up, eh?" The maid's good humor threw him off for a moment, and he looked around nervously. "Ah, you don't recognize me, then? Okay, okay. Come in. The Craven women are in the sitting room. I'll take you."

"Thank you very much, Flora." He stepped over the threshold with a looping stride.

"Ah, so you do recognize me, then," Flora said.

He cleared his throat. "I do. I'm just . . . quite nervous. I do apologize."

"No need," Flora responded, laying a hand briefly at his elbow. "It's not me you have to be nervous of."

He looked down at his feet and whispered, "Is she as terrible as they say, then?"

"Rebecca?" Flora whispered back. "Yes. But you met her, didn't you?"

"Not Mrs. Craven." Thomas looked down the hall nervously. "The girl, Mary Craven. They say she's mean-spirited and prone to fits."

Flora was immediately defensive. Mary may have been difficult to begin with, but they'd moved past that. Since the day of the temper tantrum and her subsequent breakdown in the mudroom, every day Mary came more alive. All she had needed was someone on her side, and Flora was determined to be that someone. "And now who is 'they,' Thomas March?"

He cleared his throat again. "Just, you know, they. The women—"

"I'd bet my left eyetooth, me, that the 'women' you're talking about would be Mrs. Craven herself. And probably your own maman. You never mind that gossip. Mary is a bit odd, but she's a good girl when it comes down to it." Flora turned abruptly and started up the main hall. "This way, Mr. March."

He scurried to catch up, wishing he could take back the last few minutes.

Rebecca and Mary sat in the aptly named sitting room—the elder Craven perched daintily in a wingback by the empty fireplace, the younger slouched on a flower-patterned settee.

"Mr. March for Mademoiselle," Flora announced, and stepped out of the room. She knew what place Rebecca allowed her, and it was not in the middle of family business. She retreated to the kitchen to report back to Philomene and prepare tea. "He got taller for sure, gangly even, but still has that same baby face," she'd tell her.

"Mary, stand and greet our guest," Rebecca said, not rising herself.

Mary began with a sigh, which did nothing to dispel the rumors of her bad temperament. Nevertheless, Thomas was struck by how pretty she was. She wore a navy blue dress with a crisp red bow at her neck. Her hair was dark and wavy, left to hang over her shoulders, and her face was sprinkled with light freckles like a girl of fairer complexion. And this was all pleasant enough, but it was her eyes that made him nervous. They were catlike, narrow and darting, but there was also something there that made him curious. Like her eyes had seen things that he himself might like to see.

She curtsied. "Mr. March."

"Miss Craven," he responded, holding out his hand. She took it and gave it one quick pump before letting go. Then she returned to her slump on the couch.

"Thomas, in spite of her demeanor this morning, Mary is looking forward to your visit," Rebecca said. "I've asked Flora to serve tea here. This will also be where lessons will take place. The light is good and there is plenty of room for books and such. I shall leave you to it. I have household matters to attend to, so I will be close at hand should you need me." She stood and glided out of the room.

Alone with this boy, Mary sat up a little straighter and folded her arms over her chest. She thought Rebecca would have stayed. Flora had said they probably wouldn't be left alone. Now what was she going to say?

"You live nearby?" Of course, she didn't really care, but polite conversation had to be made.

Thomas cleared his throat and sat on the wood-framed sofa opposite Mary. He set his briefcase by his feet and folded his hands in his lap. "My parents' home is in the town proper, by the church and not far from the public docks."

"I have no idea where that is. Is it far?" Mary answered.

"Haven't you been in town?" He was surprised. "But you've been here for weeks. Why would you stay all the way out here? There's nothing out here but trees and Ind—"

"Tea is served," Flora interrupted, walking in with a large round tray. "On the table there, then?"

She didn't wait for an answer and put the tray down so hard, the china clattered, giving Thomas a sidelong glance that silenced him on the subject once and for all.

"The Marches live about a half hour's ride from the manor." She answered Mary's question herself. "It's not far but might as well be for how those town folks feel about us across-the-Bay people. Enjoy your tea."

She walked out of the room on heavy feet, and tutor and pupil sat in awkward silence for a moment. Thomas's tongue was held by embarrassment. Mary was just trying not to laugh.

"I . . . I meant no offense at all. I . . . Flora Beausoleil, she is an intimidating woman, always has been," he managed, a bit of real fear on his face.

Mary picked up on this. "You knew Flora before today?"

"Indeed. I have known Flora forever, it would seem." It was then, in the remembering, that the fear on Mr. March's face turned to something else, something close to fear but with a deeper shine to it. He cleared his throat, as if to bury his own thoughts. "Now then, let's review the materials."

Eventually, they fumbled their way through serving themselves, and Thomas had pulled out his books and papers and explained the lessons they were going to tackle over the coming months. "Until you're enrolled in the school, we can take advantage of your free time," he concluded cheerfully.

"Free time?" Mary repeated. "I am actually quite busy here. Are we done for today?"

She stood up without waiting for an answer, which caused Thomas to stand so quickly he knocked a book off the low table with his knee. He stammered a bit. "S-Sure. I mean, yes. We can reconvene tomorrow."

"Fine." Mary began walking out of the room, pausing by the doorway to give a slight curtsy. "Good day, Mr. March."

He wasn't sure how to answer such a formal gesture. He clumsily put a hand at his waist and gave a slight, stilted bow, a look of confusion on his face. "Good day."

And at that, Mary left, headed to her room to change. She smirked to herself. He was a few years older than she was but was still young and lacking in confidence. His stiff little bow was a soft shadow of the way Sophie bowed, with all that pomp and ceremony to her movements. But this was good—he was no threat other than taking up more hours of her day than she'd like. But if Rebecca thought she could marry her off to this boy in a blazer, she seriously underestimated Mary's resolve. She may have also underestimated the allure of one Flora Beausoleil.

She waited for Rebecca to show up at her room, demanding an update or perhaps to quiz her, even though they'd not done any actual work. When she didn't show, Mary took out the pen and a sheet of paper and began the letter to her uncle, the one that was supposed to bring him home to put everything in order.

Beginning it was the hardest part. How does one address

a grown man whom they are related to but have never met? She hadn't even heard stories of him growing up, knew nothing of his temperament or general outlook on life. She didn't know if he was a formal man or the kind of man who would find formality off-putting. And besides all that, Mary had never before written a letter in the entirety of her life.

After a few moments of deep thought, she decided to write as if she were having a conversation with her long-lost uncle. After all, he had extended his hospitality to take her in. (She pushed the knowledge that he really had no other choice out of her mind for the time being.)

*July 23, 1901*

*Dearest Uncle,*

*Let me begin by way of introduction. I am your niece, Mary Craven, aged fifteen. I am writing to you from the desk in my room, the room you have so graciously allowed me to reside in following the tragic drowning death of my parents (and your brother and sister-in-law) aboard a less-than-sea-worthy leisure ship bound for your own homeland of England. I like to think that they made it, in the end. It helps to imagine them permanently on vacation.*

*I had the great good fortune of being left in Toronto and so avoided this fatal journey. Perhaps my parents, with the intuition parents are bound to have, sensed some kind of danger and left me in the care of my nanny in our comfortable home. Speaking now of parental intuition . . .*

*I had the life-changing opportunity to meet and spend time with darling Olive, your daughter and my only cousin. I am not, Mr. Craven, a person known for their exuberance. I am not known for anything, really, other than my tragic orphaning, though you saw fit to save me from the more tragic fate of being without care, in that respect. Olive and I, we bonded over the span of only one week, but I feel as though we were always meant to be together. I am not, of course, suggesting that my parents' dramatic oceanic demise was in any way a fortuitous event, but rather that Olive and I were sure to be brought together in this lifetime.*

*During our days together in the attic, Olive got better. I am not exaggerating when I say that she, in what I can only describe as miraculous, became bright, almost buoyant (please forgive the unfortunate nautical reference here). But it was quite a thing to bear witness to. We were even planning to produce a play together (I have taken the liberty, I should include, of borrowing a few volumes from your handsome library including a bound copy of Shakespeare's* Romeo and Juliet, *which so inspired us).*

*But what happens next in this tale is not so bright or buoyant. It is, in fact, another tragedy. Upon the return of your wife, Rebecca Craven, Olive took a turn for the worse from whence she had been sprung. (Please note, I am not suggesting any sort of connection between the two, merely pointing out the direct timeline.) Aunt Rebecca forbade any further fraternizing between us and, until very recently, I had no indication of Olive's well-being.*

*As it turns out, when I did manage to visit my dear cousin just recently, she was so poorly that I worry now for her mortal soul.*

*I hope that you do not find me out of line or take my genuine love for my cousin and concern for her well-being as nothing more than overreaction (of which, as previously mentioned, I am not known for). However, sir, I must ask that you see fit to return to Craven Manor as soon as you can. In fact, I beg of you.*

*If you should return home in quick time, you will find in myself a devoted and forever grateful niece and servant.*

*Yours dutifully,*

*Mary Craven*

She read the letter over twice, finding it at first lacking, and then on the second read entirely too much. So, she split the difference, and snuck it as-is into Flora's apron pocket at dinner to be mailed out to Detroit, where Mr. Craven was attending to business. With the letter safely in Flora's capable hands, Mary was able to eat her dinner and request to go on an evening stroll.

"Don't be out long. The mosquitoes will be on you, and bumps aren't attractive," Aunt Rebecca sniffed. She was busy poring over a catalog she'd picked up on her trip.

So Mary calmly walked through the kitchen, out the back door, and down the lawn, the picture of repose and calm. Just a young lady out to get some air, stopping to admire flowers where they were luxuriating in the end-of-day sun. But once she was in the trees, and out of eyesight from the dining room window, she ran.

There was a feeling she got now, running toward the back of the property. It was like when she broke through the willow branches on the swing. It was like nothing she could really describe. She wouldn't dare try. She didn't like to sound like a fool, and there was no way to describe it without sounding even a little foolish. But it was like shedding something and also like putting something on.

She forgot about things like her parents and her uncle's wife and even that Olive was sick. All of that went away. And instead, she felt the muscles stretch and flex in her legs. She felt the way her hair bounced lightly against her back when she moved. She wanted to touch everything around her instead of recoil from its dirt and scent. She wondered if this was what Sophie meant all the time when she spoke about home, about being home, about belonging to a place.

*Me, I'm never bored. Never lonely neither. There's just too much*, she'd told Mary.

It reminded her of Flora explaining how the wild wasn't empty. For a thing to be wild, it had to be full. It had to be crowded, even if it was with things you couldn't find the right words to label.

She pushed through the trees and wandered down to the shore. There was no point in going to the garden. Sophie wouldn't be there this late, and the garden didn't have the same magic without Sophie in it, waiting for her with that great big smile.

---

When young Mr. March showed up the next morning, Rebecca left straightaway.

"I have to head into town. Perhaps I'll stop in on your mother, Thomas," she said.

The boy's cheeks flushed a bit. "I'm sure she'd be delighted."

Mary caught the tone in his voice. She waited until the front door closed before speaking. "Your mother doesn't like my aunt, does she?"

If she had pinched him above his knee, he couldn't have reacted more than he did to these words. "Oh! Why would you say that? Of course she likes her. She likes her just fine."

Mary leaned back in the couch so that her shoulders were slumped and her head rested on the back cushions. "It's okay. I don't like her either. She's not my blood aunt. She's not even the first Mrs. Craven. I think I would have liked her."

"You really are a different kind of girl, aren't you?"

"How so?"

"Well, most ladies don't say things like that," he continued. "Not out loud in company, at least."

"Maybe you need to meet some new ladies, then." Mary had no nerves about this boy. In fact, she was determined to be exactly herself. If she had learned anything from her own mother, it was that she was a very unlikable girl. So just being herself, she felt, would afford her the safety of being uncourtable.

She had a sudden thought that made her sit up straight. "Thomas?"

"Mmm?" He was busy sorting through his papers for today's lesson on *avoir* and *aller*.

"Do you know anything about medicine?"

"No, not really." He licked his finger to flip pages.

"Science, then?"

"No." He finally looked up. "Why the sudden interest in other subjects?"

She slumped back into half recline. "No reason."

There was a voice in the hallway—someone was singing a song about a small cat and a cabbage. It didn't make sense to Mary, but then again her French was not very good (hence Mr. March). They both looked toward the doorway.

Flora sauntered in, finally free from the scrutinizing gaze of Rebecca. She saw Thomas and folded her arms over her chest. "Oh, are you here again?"

There was that high color in his cheeks once more. Mary smirked. "Yes, Flora. Thomas is coming to visit me every day. Aren't you, Mr. March?"

The boy snatched the small glasses off his face and sat straighter, if that was even possible. "Yes. Mrs. Craven has asked that our lessons take place—"

Flora laughed, waving him off. "Oh, I don't care. It was just a comment. I don't need your work schedule." She turned to Mary. "You need drinks in here, now?"

"Yes, I will have a bourbon, and Mr. Thomas would like . . ." She tapped a finger on her chin. "Brandy. He looks like a brandy man to me."

"But I don't drink!" He fairly shouted it.

Flora laughed. "Not much funny business in your household, eh? So, two ice teas, then?"

"No," Mary answered for the both of them. "We're all right. But you know, Flora, I could do with a partner in this."

"Partner?"

"Oui, mademoiselle." She exaggerated the accent. "You are French, and me? Well, I am just an English girl from an English-speaking city. I get so embarrassed by my terrible pronunciation. Could you sit with us and maybe lend some expertise?"

Flora's eyebrows lifted. "Oh really?"

"Yes, really," Mary said sweetly. "Please?"

"You want me to sit in on your tutoring sessions? But my French, it's not the same as his French," she said, pointing her thumb at Thomas. "I speak half-breed, me."

"But it's not much different," Mary replied. "The words sound the same, you just . . . say them a bit different."

"Ha!" Flora forced a laugh. She did seem a bit sheepish about it. Mary wasn't used to seeing the older girl rattled or not sure of herself in any way. "We don't speak proper. My Mère, she would call our way 'good Français.' But I don't think Thomas wants to hear all that. Might upset his lessons."

"It would be no bother at all," Thomas answered, a little too rushed. He stood to offer her the better half of the settee, and a bundle of pages fell to the rug. He dropped to his knees to collect them. Over his hunched back, Flora shot Mary a look that told her she knew the girl was up to something. Mary just smiled back, like the loveliest child in the world.

"Don't think this is gonna mess with your learning, you," Flora warned before smoothing out the back of her skirts and sitting. "I'm not staying the whole time."

"Any time you do stay would be just . . . ," Thomas began and then caught himself. "Would be very useful for Mary, Miss Beausoleil. Very instructive in the local vernacular."

She gave him an odd look, as if he had something on his face. When he didn't continue, she opened her eyes wider. "Well, aren't you going to start, then?"

He gave a quick jump. For a moment it looked like his pages were going to end up on the floor again. "Ah, yes."

Flora stayed in the sitting room for almost an hour. In that time, Mary didn't learn a single thing, other than the fact that Thomas and Flora had both grown up in the area and remembered seeing each other in town. Thomas reminded her that she gave him a bloody nose once when he bumped into her little sister in town and the smaller girl had fallen on her backside and began to cry.

"Was that Sophie?" It was one of the few times Mary interrupted, not wanting them to really remember she was there at all.

"Ah, it was!" Flora laughed. "She was tough even that tiny, but this brute took her by surprise. And she got her dress dirty in the mud, poor bébé."

"It was an accident!" Thomas cried. "One I paid for dearly, mind you. And I guarantee that it was harder to clean the blood off my shirt than the dirt off a pink pinafore. I got another beating when I went home like that, let me tell you."

Flora made a small noise, like the sound one would make at a baby who was fussing. Then she placed a hand on his elbow. Thomas looked like he might jump out of his skin at her touch. Flora did not miss his reaction.

"A pink dress?" Mary was so caught up in this small detail she forgot the game that was playing out in front of her, at her behest, even. Sophie in a dress? It was too odd to imagine.

When the grandfather clock in the hallway chimed the

noon hour, it was Flora's turn to stand abruptly. Thomas tried to stand just as quick. Good manners insisted upon a gentleman standing when a lady does. Of course, he dropped a book in his rush.

"Dieu! I haven't made lunch." She rushed off in a swirl of skirts.

Once again, it was just Thomas and Mary in the room, and the prospect of actually having to get some work done was looming. Luckily, Philomene had prepared the noon meal in Flora's absence, and with Mrs. Craven still gone, the four of them sat together at the dining room table.

"Tell me more about Sophie as a child," Mary insisted before digging into her plate of ham. "Did she always wear dresses?"

The rest of the visit passed pleasantly, until Rebecca returned and snuffed out any prospect of fun. But Mary had seen enough already.

---

"Your sister is in love!"

Mary came dancing into the garden, swaying in a kind of clumsy one-woman waltz. Sophie watched her for a while, bemused by both her friend's mood and her choreography.

"What's this nonsense? Which sister?"

“The only one I know, silly.” Mary danced over to Sophie where she stood brushing soil off her knees from working the ground around the succulents. Mary grabbed her hands and pulled her into her shuffling loops, spinning them both round and round. “Flora is in love. And it is the sweetest thing!”

“Merde!” Sophie spat. “There’s no way my sister has time for a boy. She’s been sixty since she was six.”

“Not merde,” Mary answered, laughing at her own words. “I saw it myself. She even giggled.”

“No!”

“Oui!”

They swung so wildly, they ended up in a low cedar bush. But even that didn’t stop them talking about this exciting new development. “With that schoolteacher?”

“Thomas is just a tutor. He’s much too young and much too nervous to be an actual teacher. Teachers are stern. He’s just . . . sweet,” Mary answered, climbing back to her feet and straightening out her clothes.

“Sweet, eh?” Sophie’s voice was low. “Are you sure it’s not you in love, then?”

If Mary didn’t know any better, she would think Sophie sounded jealous. It was a thought that didn’t upset her. In fact, she kind of liked it. “I have no use for Mr. Thomas March, other than to match him up with our dear Flora.”

"Hmph. Well then. We'll see, I s'pose." Sophie pulled her cap down tight over her braids. "I thought you were dancing in here 'cause your uncle wrote back."

Remembering the letter brought reality pouring into the garden. Mary's face fell. She felt the weight of the situation with her cousin and the weight of guilt that she had forgotten about it—even if just for a moment.

"No. Not yet. Flora says it could take a week, even with the extra postage she paid. I'm hoping the new medicine does the trick."

"I have something to show you, come." She held her hand out, and Mary took it.

They walked under the willow branches. "Look, the second swing, she's up."

And it was. There, a few small feet from each other, hung the two swings. Mary wondered if they were close enough that the riders could clasp hands while they flew.

"Oh, it's so lovely!" Mary meant it. Maybe it was the quick switch from joy to worry and then back to joy that was too much, because her eyes filled up with tears. And Mary Craven was no crier. Other than the incident in the mudroom, she hadn't shed a tear in as long as she could remember.

"Oh no!" Sophie grabbed Mary by the shoulders and stooped to look in her eyes closely. "I've brought on this? Ah Jesus. I'm so sorry, Mary. I didn't mean to talk about the letter. I was just feeling twisted about the English boy."

Mary opened her mouth to ask what she meant by twisted, but nothing came out. Her throat was hitching, and if she didn't close her mouth, she would have sobbed. Just then, Sophie pulled her in close, bringing her face against her shoulder. The sudden warmth of her body through the men's shirt, the tightness of her arms around her, the rise and fall of her breathing—together it all shook the tears loose, and Mary rested there, being held, fully held in a way she had never been held.

Sophie was speaking to her, the words in French but the cadence perfectly understandable. Mary was being cared for. It was a kindness that changed the nature of the tears but kept them coming, and Mary closed her eyes and was just a girl being held for a moment. She felt acutely aware of that connection, all the points of contact between them.

And then the strangest thing happened.

It felt as if the sound had shifted around them, or maybe it was just the garden slowly growing in a long, green exhale. But all at once, Mary felt better, more than better. She felt a deep connection—to Sophie, to this place, to herself. It was a feeling of calm that stopped her crying and made her reach to wrap her own arms around Sophie. She opened her eyes and all around them there was connection. This was their place. They had created this space. Not the original creators, but still, they had made it what it was now, and there was nowhere in the wide world that could feel better than to be here. But, she realized when the thought of pulling away was painful, *right* here, in Sophie's arms.

It was the moment that Mary Craven realized that she was in love.

"You ready to swing?" Sophie asked, her voice coming from her mouth and through her chest at the same time.

"Just a moment longer," Mary whispered. "Just a little longer . . ."

# 14

# As Boundless as the Sea

The next few days for Mary were a blur of French lessons and finding excuses for Flora to join them, then rushing to the garden to work and play and to try to find excuses to be physically close to Sophie. But in between and over top of everything else was her worry for Olive in the attic.

On this front, Mary received a reprieve on the day Aunt Rebecca got hurt, which felt, in more ways than one, like there was help coming from somewhere just past the stars.

---

A few rapid knocks at the door echoed through the first floor.

Rebecca leapt up from the breakfast table so fast she knocked over her glass of milk. "They're here!"

Mary, not used to any sort of outburst from the woman, sat dumbfounded while Rebecca scampered out of the room and clacked down the hall in her narrow-heeled boots, watching the thick liquid pool drip onto the floor. Finally, she got up, sidestepped the mess, and wandered into the hallway to see what the fuss was about.

Flora was unlatching the top lock on the second door so that two large men could enter carrying a wooden crate—tall and wide but thin, as if it were a gigantic book. Rebecca, more composed in front of guests, stood wringing her hands off to the side.

Still, being Rebecca, she couldn't help but bark orders.

"This way, careful of the walls. That's very expensive paper. I had it brought in from New York, you see. Over here, now."

She walked them to the foot of the stairs. "Now, first things first, you'll need to remove this. It's to be rehung in the attic."

"Madame, we don't have instructions for removal and installation," the taller man with a large, almost comical mustache said.

"What do you mean? How else am I going to hang it?"

The man shrugged, holding onto the bib of his overalls and surreptitiously eyeing Flora as she rebolted the door. "Reach out to the office, I suppose."

"No," Rebecca said. Mary recognized her tone as the one she used when she was trying to hold back her anger. It was overly calm, like the breeze before a storm. "I sat for three days for this portrait. Spent a fortune on custom framing. Had it shipped at great cost. Now, I demand that it be installed. Right now. Immediately."

The second man was already making his escape, back onto the front porch. He moved quietly for such a large man. Still, he did not evade notice.

"Ah, ah, you there!" Rebecca pointed at him—another sign that her anger was reaching dangerous levels, as ladies did not point. "Unless you are going to the wagon to get tools, you get back in here this instant and hang this picture!"

He just shrugged and hurried down the steps to their carriage. The horses snuffed and fidgeted, ready to assist in the retreat.

"Listen, we have other deliveries to make. What can I say, I'm not the management, just the courier," the first man said, holding out a slip of paper.

Rebecca crossed her arms over her chest and glared.

He sighed, turned, and handed it to Flora. He tipped

his hat to the room and left. Within a minute, the sound of heavy hooves and rolling wheels made their way up the long drive to the front gate.

"I won't stand for this!" Rebecca shouted. Though, at this point, she was just talking to herself. "Flora, where is Jean?"

"He's on his day off, Madame. Back in community." Flora was sweeping up the foyer floor, knowing damn well that's what would be demanded of her once Rebecca returned to her normal, terrible senses. She hated the thought of "other people's dirt" being tracked into her house.

Rebecca threw her hands up and let them fall back at her sides dramatically. "Well then, there'll be no getting him now. Probably drunk on corn liquor and gut rot."

"Corn liquor?" Flora was not usually moved by the casual racism thrown about the house, but she was confused by this detail.

"At any rate, here we are." Rebecca hung her head, her hand to her forehead as though she had suddenly been struck with a headache.

Mary tried to emulate the second delivery man, creeping behind her to the stairs. She had one foot on the bottom step when she was summoned.

"Well, I suppose we can pretend to be a part of those wild suffrage women and just do the damn work ourselves. Mary? Go to the shed and get the tool box."

———

They managed to take down the first Mrs. Craven's portrait easily enough. It was heavy and a bit awkward, but with Flora on one side and Mary on the other (with Rebecca directing), it was not a difficult job.

"Just lay it there, against the step, not the wall. You know that's—"

"Expensive wallpapering," Mary finished for her. "We know."

"Right," Rebecca said, oblivious to the annoyance in the girl's voice. "It is indeed. Now, open the crate. There must be a crowbar or wrench or something in the box."

"How's a wrench—?" Mary cut herself off. Why bother? She sorted through the heavy metal tools until she found a small pry bar. Flora took it and began the work of pulling at the nails holding the new package together. When the last one popped, Rebecca rushed in.

"Open it, open it!" she ordered excitedly.

Flora lifted the top and set it aside, then reached in to clear off the packing hay that held the gilded frame safely in its container.

"Oh!" Rebecca put both hands to her mouth. "Oh my."

Mary was suddenly curious. She walked over and looked into the box. Upon seeing it, she wasn't sure if her aunt's reaction was one of horror or delight.

There was a portrait in there, all right, but who it was of, well, that was a mystery. The woman in the painting wore a deep red gown, corseted across the front like early nobility, with a sheer bodice piece that did nothing to hide a very ample bosom squeezing out of the tight fabric. Above the mounds of rounded flesh was a stiff lace collar that reached her chin with a scalloped edge adorned with dangling pearls. Her skin was very pale, almost as white as the collar piece. Her hands were laid one over the other on what appeared to be a high table or a mantel of some sort just out of range at the bottom of the portrait. Each finger was overly long and adorned with a ruby-encrusted ring. Her face was serene and proud, her gaze fixed somewhere in the middle distance as if she were to be admired and not to engage with the viewer in any way. Her cheekbones were high and her mouth was a bright pink rosebud, smaller than any human's mouth could ever be. The whole shape of her face gave the idea of a St. Valentine's Day heart, coming to a dimpled point.

But where the face was petite, almost too diminutive, the hair was massive. On top of that pale heart was a pile of strawberry curls, tendrils escaping to touch her bare shoulders. Here and there, strands of pearls were draped so that the entire hairstyle became a sort of crown. Topping it off was an ornate pearl and diamond headpiece, like a broach mistakenly placed, from which a large red ostrich plume exploded, filling the rest of the space into the upper right corner.

"Who is that?" Mary asked.

"Isn't it lovely?" Rebecca approached the open box with shaking hands held out in front of her. She hadn't heard her niece's query. In fact, she seemed in a world wholly to herself. "Oh, it's even better than I could have imagined."

Mary looked over to Flora and shrugged. The maid pinched her lips between her teeth, trying to hold in her laughter.

"I look divine!" Rebecca squealed. "Like Marie Antoinette herself." She wiped at her eyes and clapped her hands together, turning to face the silent girls. "We need to get this up right away. I can't wait another minute!"

They freed the portrait from the box and lugged it over to the space it was to take up, replacing the first Mrs. Craven with the second. It was heavy and took some doing. They inched it over with small steps. It was easily two times the size of the original painting, and the frame was ornate, carved with small bundles of golden fruit and lush florals. Lifting it to catch the wires onto the hook in the wall was a real struggle and took three tries.

"Come on now, and don't scrape the wall!" Rebecca was like a child waiting for a new toy to be unpackaged.

When it was finally up and Rebecca had given a dozen conflicting directions on which way to "jostle it" so that it was straight, Flora spoke up. "Madame, I don't think it's good."

"What do you mean, of course it is." Rebecca closed one

eye and squinted at it. "It's perfectly straight now, finally. It's like you girls were *trying* to make it crooked."

"No, no. I mean, the hook. It's too petite."

"Nonsense." Rebecca strode over to the wall. "You don't know anything about art, and certainly nothing about home structure. Maybe your shack is flimsy, but Craven Manor? No, it's fine. Such a delicate portrait. It doesn't need more than—"

And that's when the hook pulled straight out of the wall, and the hideous portrait of a strange woman with tiny lips and enormous hair came crashing to the floor.

Or more precisely, it came crashing directly on top of Rebecca's foot.

There were a few seconds of silence after the *bang*. Flora and Mary made eye contact and waited . . . And then came the howls.

Rebecca hopped about with her arms flapping so wildly it was hard to take it seriously. Then she sat flat on her bottom on the floor and clutched the smashed foot, rocking back and forth, tears now streaming down her face. The girls jumped into action, helping her to the parlor, sitting her on the couch, and unlacing her heeled boot—all the while taking the barrage of curses that streamed over them.

Philomene was summoned from the kitchen by the commotion and, after examining the foot, set about gathering the herbs and wrap she needed to help with the swelling and pain.

"I need a doctor, not a witch!" Rebecca screamed.

Just then, there was a knock at the door.

"That'll be Tho—Mr. March," Flora said. Mary noticed she patted down her hair and smoothed out the front of her dress.

"Get me to the kitchen!" Rebecca shrieked. The thought of being embarrassed over an exposed foot and a messy face got her to stand and hobble up the hallway, her arm slung over Flora's shoulders as a crutch.

"Well, I guess that'll be me, then," Mary mumbled, opening the front door.

"What's going on? I heard crying from the porch?" Thomas was looking around Mary and caught the women at the end of the hallway. "Is something wrong? Did something happen to Flora?"

Mary couldn't help but smirk at his query. Of course he was frantic, because he thought it was Flora who had called out.

"No, no. It's just my aunt. A painting fell on her foot." She indicated the portrait now laying on its side against the wall.

Thomas turned his head to the side and examined it. "Who is that?"

Mary smiled. Maybe today was going to be a good day after all.

---

The lesson flew by quickly. They weren't being watched and Flora was unavailable, so they spent some time just talking about life in general in between subjugating verbs and counting *en Français*. Thomas, as it turned out, had known Flora and Sophie's Père.

"He was the best canoesman in these parts. My father used to ask him to test out the new boats before he'd put them in inventory. Sometimes they argued, but that man, he refused to compromise when he thought a craft wasn't worth its hull."

"I see where her stubbornness comes from, then," Mary said, more to herself than Thomas.

"Who, Flora? Yes, she is strong-willed."

"No, Sophie. Her sister," Mary said. "The baby in the pink dress you threw down?"

"For the last time, I did not throw her down. I bumped into her!"

"Whatever, same result. Where do they live, anyway?"

"Not far from here. They're with the other across-the-Bay people, the ones who came from the Island and some from out west and some made their way from Indian Territory across the border," he explained. "They live pretty close together, though the land's being sold around them, and some families are starting to leave the shore."

"Being pushed away from it, is how it is," Flora's voice cut in. She walked into the parlor and sat heavily on the arm of the settee, sighing. "Mon dieu, that woman can fuss."

Thomas was startled and a little embarrassed to have been

caught talking about her, but he rallied. "How is Mrs. Craven, anyhow?"

"Oh, she'll live," Flora answered. "Nothing broken, but you wouldn't know from the carrying on."

"Sounded like she was going to have to get it cut off," Mary interjected. "I suppose we'll have to do everything for her for a while, until she decides she's not an invalid anymore."

"That's true," Flora said, standing once more. "Like right now, I have to go upstairs and tend to her lunchtime duties." She spoke slowly, keeping eye contact with Mary who quickly caught on.

She sprung up, knowing this could only mean one thing—the attic. "I'll help!"

"Non, you have to go eat in the dining room now. But I will see you after and let you know how the . . . duties went."

Mary was simultaneously elated and disappointed. "Are you sure I can't help? Thomas won't mind."

"Oui. She is waiting for you in there. Get ready to hear all about her injury, both of you. She's already made it bigger than the American War."

It was true. They spent almost an hour hearing all about Rebecca's foot, about the things that Flora and Mary did wrong that facilitated such a tragedy. "If they'd only held it so I could check the hook, but they were so eager to let it go, as if they hadn't enough strength to hold it. Impatience, really. I thought all along that it wasn't going to hold," she told Thomas.

Mary let her prattle on, barely eating more than a few spoonfuls of tomato soup, waiting for Flora's return. She turned a few times to check the doorway until she was scolded. "Mary Craven, why are you so fidgety today? It's very unbecoming in a young lady, especially when we have a young gentleman over."

Mary, who was getting better at understanding the nature of her aunt, responded. "I'm just all twisted sideways about your accident, Aunt Rebecca. It's bothered my composure today, I guess. And my concentration."

"Hmm. Perhaps we should call today's lesson short, then," Rebecca said, clearly touched by the girl's obvious sympathy and also wanting to get to her bed and take some of the laudanum drops she kept in her dresser. "Yes, we can end right after lunch."

With adequate motivation, Mary was sipping the last dregs of her soup when Rebecca passed by and into the kitchen.

"Flora!" Rebecca called out. "Flora, see Mr. March to the door and then help me to my room. I need to rest my leg."

"Your leg now, is it?" Flora answered, but with a pleasant enough tone that Rebecca didn't pick up on the sarcasm. She appeared at the door. "Right away, Madame. Mr. March, this way please."

As they were walking down the hallway, Rebecca changed

subjects from her own misery. "So, Mary. How are lessons going?"

"Oh, good," Mary answered. "J'apprends beaucoup."

By her expression, it became clear that while she espoused the benefits of a "proper lady" having more than one language with which to entertain her husband's guests, Rebecca Craven did not understand a word of French. "That's . . . good. Very good. And how are things progressing with Mr. March?"

"Progressing? Why, he's an excellent teacher, if that's what you mean."

"That is not what I mean." Rebecca sighed at the girl's simplemindedness. "He comes from a good family, you know. His father has amassed a quiet fortune here, and they are from fine English stock."

"Madame?" Flora had returned. "Let's get you up into bed."

"Careful now. I am quite fragile in this state," she answered, using the table to brace herself before leaning all her weight on the maid. Flora took it all in stride, but her face was a bit flushed from effort.

Nevertheless, she stopped beside Mary's chair. "Miss, you have a bit of food on your chin, there. Here—" She dug into the pocket of her apron. "Use this hankie to clean it off."

Mary was already swiping at her chin with the back of her hand when the handkerchief was placed in front of her. She noticed that the little square was embroidered. Must be one of Flora's own. She picked it up as the women limped out into the hall and gasped.

As it unfolded, she could clearly see that it had indeed been embroidered, and she recognized the pattern—precise green leaves spiraled out from a circular tangle of vines, and in the center were three letters—HTC. And underneath the design was a line of text:

***As Boundless as the Sea***

A quote from *Romeo and Juliet*. But the part that made Mary's breath catch, the thing that made her heart quicken was that the needlepoint—without question—had been done by Olive.

# 15

# The Final Words

"We have to celebrate!" Mary hadn't put the needlepoint down since Flora had slipped it to her. She'd examined the careful stitches, ran her fingers over the even rows, and read the message a dozen times already. "It worked. It really worked!"

"Are you sure?" Sophie had been waiting in the garden, not expecting Mary to arrive so soon, and certainly not expecting her to come running in like she was being chased by Satan himself.

"I asked Flora after she put Rebecca to bed. She said Olive is feeling much better. Look!" She held the handkerchief up again. "She was able to do this. She's back to herself."

"So what do we do now?" Sophie allowed herself to feel a bit of relief. She didn't take much comfort in things that happened in the world that was beyond her reach; you could never really know what went on in white homes. But Olive was a Trudeau, and the Trudeaus were cousins of the Beausoleils. In some ways, that made it harder to be completely overjoyed like Mary. When half-breeds got caught up in the other world, *their* world, they were always vulnerable.

"Flora is worried about keeping it secret," Mary conceded. In fact, Flora had been full of nerves about the whole thing when they'd spoken.

"I'm not sure Olive can hide it," Sophie said. "I told her to stay put, to be quiet, but . . . must be hard. We have to keep this up until Monsieur returns. Until he can free her."

"Why?" Mary could barely keep her voice down, she was so full of excitement.

"Why? Because who knows what that woman will do next? We don't know if that medicine being bad was a mistake or a plan. Non, that kwe needs to wait for her pa to come home." She passed her look over Mary, who was practically buzzing. "We all need to wait."

Now even Sophie was being cautious—it was maddening. Mary needed to do something with all this happiness or she would burst. And then it came to her, the way they could do something while they did nothing at all.

"I have an idea . . ."

---

Flora wanted to stay out of it.

She was waiting just as impatiently for word from Mr. Craven as Mary was. When Mr. Craven was at home, he mostly stayed in his quarters, shuffling to his office in the morning and back to his rooms at dark, every now and then taking his meals at the dining table instead of his desk. But the second Mrs. Craven? At least when her husband was home, she was distracted a bit and made an effort to appear kind to the staff in front of him. But when he was out of earshot, things returned to normal, and she ruled over every inch of the manor with a keen eye and a sharp tongue.

*This piano couldn't play even if there was someone around clever enough to do so. The weight of the dust wouldn't allow the keys to move!*

*Are we that lazy? Or are we assuming curtain rods are not susceptible to grime? Take them down and soak them. Wash the drapes while you're at it.*

*This tea is too strong! Are you trying to choke me? Less tea, more water. How many times must I repeat myself?*

So when Sophie and Mary requested Flora's help in finding the right clothes to make costumes and in gathering enough lanterns to light up a large section of the back property, Flora had pause. "I'm not sure that's a good idea. What if she notices, her? The missing clothes? The lanterns?

And what if those lanterns turn while you're dancin' around and the grass catches? She will whip us all, and you know better than anyone, Sophie, how I need to keep this job. For Maman, for the kids."

"Aw, come on, Flora. If anyone can make magic happen, it's you," Sophie sweet-talked, grabbing onto her older sister's arm and looking up with wide eyes. "Besides, by the time the play is ready, Craven'll be back, and Mary is gonna take care of him."

"How? He hasn't even met her yet," Flora said. "You have that much belief in your charms, eh? That you can charm a stranger into listening to you swamp rats like your doctors that know best?"

"Yes, I am that confident. One can be confident when they have the truth on their side," Mary said, mimicking Sophie by grabbing Flora's other arm. "And what could go wrong with a play? After all, it's going to be a celebration of Olive's return to health. We are throwing it in her honor. And if anyone can help, it's you. From the day we met, I thought 'now this girl, this girl is a patron of the arts if I've ever seen one.'"

Flora was worn down pretty quick. "Oh *saint tonne le vie*, why did I ever put the likes of you two together?" She shrugged them off her, Mary blushing from the thought of being together with Sophie. "We don't even know when Craven will come back, when he got that damned letter. And we don't know that Olive is getting better for real this time."

But it was impossible to deny these two, especially Mary. She was so different from the girl who had rode up, sullen and hard, to the gates that spring. Flora paced a few steps, sighed, resigned to her fate, then turned on the girls, finger raised.

"You better keep all your . . . your *merde*"—she struggled to find a word other than a simple cuss—"you keep it away from here. You can't get caught with the clothes or the lanterns or any of it. She'll brand you thieves. And then the devil himself won't be able to help you." She made a quick sign of the cross over her chest and stormed back inside.

As soon as the screen door bounced against its frame, Sophie and Mary grabbed each other's hands and twirled in a circle, faster and faster, laughing. Sophie's braids whipped out behind her, and Mary's dress caught the wind and ballooned out about her knees.

"We're going to have a play! Long live the the-a-ter," Mary cried out in a bad British accent.

"Indeed we are." Sophie tried to copy her forced tone. "Indeed, indeed!"

They fell to the grass, dizzy and tired, giggling through their smiles. Heads beside one another, Sophie turned to look at her friend. "Mary?"

"Hmm?" Mary kept her eyes on a fat cloud above them, trying to stop the spinning in her head. She also didn't want to look at Sophie. It was getting harder to look at her without wanting something else that she didn't have words for. Besides, lying this way, she could feel the push of the girl's breath moving the small hairs at her temple. It made her stomach feel light, full of small bilious wings.

"What play are we gonna do, anyway?"

Mary's smile faltered. "You know what play we're going to do, the only one we know. The one Olive wants us to do."

---

First, they needed to read through the play, then they would work on assigning roles and rehearsing. Mary had called Juliet from that first afternoon, and Sophie was happy to take on Romeo, even though she thought he was weak.

For the next four days, French lessons were had, Rebecca was cared for, and the house was happy. They knew Olive was getting better, and with Rebecca shut in her bedroom, the original trio of Philomene, Mary, and Flora were able to eat their meals together in peace. Mr. March joined them for lunches, of course, and his laughter joined theirs. They loved teasing him and he took it all in stride. By that Friday, he was pitching in to clear the table and had stopped wearing his jacket in the house. It felt, for the first time, like a family lived in the manor.

Rebecca insisted on going up to "tend to Olive," but Flora

went with her, carrying the trays and acting as a living crutch. At least she was able to share news from the attic this way.

"The medicine is almost done," Flora told them at dinner. We'll have to make a new batch soon enough if Monsieur Craven doesn't get back."

"Maybe the conception was a mistake?" Mary suggested quietly. "Rebecca doesn't seem like she'd know dill from a daisy . . ."

"Perhaps," Flora conceded. "But we cannot take the chance. What if she made no mistake? What happens when she knows and decides to give the girl something else, something worse?"

Philomene spoke then, but it was in a dialect Mary couldn't translate.

"What did she say?"

Flora kept Philomene's glance for a beat, then nodded. "She says, some women, they prefer their children when they're smaller, when they're needy. For most, it's because they want to be needed, to keep caring for them as if they're bébés forever. For others it's because they want to be the hero—the martyr, like at the Shrine, the one people worship for their sacrifice. At any cost, then, the child stays small."

"And which kind is Aunt Rebecca?" Mary asked, but she wasn't sure she wanted the answer.

"Tous les deux," Philomene said.

"Both," Mary repeated in English. "Sounds . . . dangerous."

"So, we wait for Monsieur," Flora concluded. "We keep an eye on the fille, and we wait."

---

Saturday and Sunday were free days, and with her aunt still hobbling around, Mary was free to spend all her hours outside. She felt odd starting the preparations for the play without Olive, but there was nothing to be done for it, not yet. She would find a way to include Olive soon enough. But in the meantime, they needed to study the words and scenes as best they could. Over the span of two days, she and Sophie had gotten through most of the play. Mary read while Sophie worked, as she wanted it.

"I like moving, me," she'd explained. "Helps me think. I can see it better this way."

So while the story spun itself out, the garden was cleared and weeded and trimmed. Under capable hands and a knowing mind, it had become the most beautiful of all the gardens. They knew that for a fact since they took breaks from work and reading to explore the other six unlocked, less remarkable gardens.

"I feel sorry for this one," Mary had said, standing in the doorway of the walled area closest to the western greenhouse. "It's the shorter, plainer sister to ours."

Sophie laughed. Her crow followed them on these journeys. He seemed to agree with the overall assessment, cawing indifferently from the stunted trees and plain walls that were not allowed to be cloaked in climbing vines. He refused to even steal the offerings in these gardens, leaving seeds and berries and sweet nuts where he found them. It was a relief to always return to their own space, the one they had spent all summer cultivating.

"Bay Blooms, these ones," Sophie commented, watering the base of a large rosebush.

"Oh, are they roses from here?" Mary liked learning more about this land.

"They are now," Sophie replied. "And they need a name that claims them."

"Bay Blooms," Mary repeated. "I like it."

By Sunday night, they were exhausted from the work and the planning of their performance. Even in that exhaustion, Mary felt the nervous energy that she found herself addicted to, the way being with Sophie made her notice things like the abundance of stars or the perfect shapes that could be found in nature all around them. Sometimes, she thought she could understand why people went to church—maybe they were looking for this feeling, the feeling that nothing this great could be random, that there was a design. And hers could only be complete in these moments, with this girl. So, sitting on their swings, slightly twisting as if they were tall daisies in the breeze, Mary read and Sophie listened as the story of *Romeo and Juliet* came to its sad conclusion.

*"A glooming peace this morning with it brings. The sun, for sorrow, will not show his head. Go hence, to have more talk of these sad things. Some shall be pardoned, and some punished."*

Mary closed the book with a sigh. She felt a weight pressing on her eyes and throat. She had read this book before, of course, but now it carried this with it—some kind of weight that made her physically react.

"It's so sad," she said, not much louder than a whisper. "And romantic."

"It's horrible," Sophie said.

"Yes, so tragic, what happened."

"No," she said a little more forcefully. "It's a horrible story."

The spell over Mary was broken, and she looked at Sophie, who had stood and had put her hands on her hips. "What? How could you say that?"

"'Cause I think it, I know it. Who dies for love?"

Mary felt a danger in the air. Was this one of those moments when your ideas about someone, your *feelings* about them, all change? "Maybe we should read it again. You must have missed something."

"Non, I missed nothing. Why do you think it has to be me who missed a thing, not you? Not William?"

Mary scoffed. "Because I know this play inside and out.

And because William Shakespeare wrote the story, and he is a master."

"Says who?"

Mary threw her arms up and out, indicating the entirety of the world around them. "Everyone!"

"Not me." Sophie sat back down on the swing and took a few steps backward with the wood seat across her bottom, ready to launch. "You put too much stock in men who other men say are good, are right. Why do their words matter and not mine?"

Mary maneuvered her swing so that she was blocking Sophie's path. She couldn't loosen her feet to take to the sky without smashing into her first. There was no getting out of this debate now, certainly not by swinging away.

"We learn the classics for a reason."

"And what's that?" Sophie huffed, annoyed that her path was now cut off. She released the rope and put her hands in her lap, held still by her feet in the dirt.

"Because they are the best we have. The best of mankind. It makes us better to know them." Mary thought this was all so simple. But something began to loosen in her as she spoke.

"They are what, England's best? This is not England. This is not where English words shape the land. English doesn't hold us. Here, we hold it, and that means it cannot hold our best," Sophie spoke slowly, as if she were explaining a complex theory to a simple child, and in many ways, she was.

At least where stories and this place were concerned. When Mary didn't respond, she continued.

"I ask, why do you die for love? Because that's not what love wants."

Mary narrowed her eyes, thinking and feeling a bit vulnerable now. "Then what does it want? Tell me? Because I know less about love than anything, ever. I don't know love, so tell me."

Just then, Sophie grasped the ropes, released her feet, and came careening toward her. There was no time to move; she was so surprised at the sudden motion. Mary braced for impact and closed her eyes. And then Sophie's body collided with hers, but without violence. She had dragged a foot and grabbed the ropes of Mary's swing, pulling her in. Now the girls were together in a tangle, face-to-face, Sophie's breath on Mary's cheek.

"Love, cherie, love wants us to live. You live for love." Her voice was low, from somewhere in her throat or the sky or even in the tree they dangled from, suspended now against each other, turning slow like one single bloom.

"Love wants everything but death."

Without opening her eyes, Mary instinctively pushed her face forward, unable to breathe, unable to exist outside of this connection. And her lips were met by lips.

She pulled back a bit and gasped. Because that was when she knew exactly what love's intentions were—everything.

Then she leaned back in, lips slightly apart, and found Sophie's again. They hung there, two girls sharing the first kiss of their lives, suspended in the sky, and everything else faded away—her parents, her loneliness, her entire solitary life. She left everything else behind in the shadows where they belonged, and leaned into this light.

Because, sometimes, even in the darkness, if you just push hard enough, you can end up sailing into the bright open.

———

Sophie had walked her to the back door. They didn't talk, just made small connections across the lawn—shoulders bumping, the back of a hand grazing an arm, a shared look. It was the longest and briefest of walks. Under the deeper shadow of the manor's back wall, the crickets were loudest, like tiny drummers calling the army of the evening to take back this colonized space, to tear down the panels and release the ground once more.

They were unsure of how to say goodbye, feeling certain that there was no way for them to exist as separate beings now that they were together. The thought of going inside, putting one of these walls between them, made Mary panic.

"I don't want to go inside," she admitted.

"I don't want you to go inside," Sophie agreed. "We could leave now, us. Live in the bush. No." She laughed. "You're a city lady. I could fix up the Old Fort. Use that as a house. Have chickens for eggs. Teach you to fish."

It was Mary's turn to laugh, but she didn't. "I could learn." She was very serious.

"Okay, cherie. You go in. I have to get home before my mother hollers. But I'll be here tomorrow."

"Early? Will you come early? I'll try to convince Thomas to cut it short." Mary felt desperate. She even grabbed Sophie's hand, then got shy. "If you want to."

Sophie squeezed her hand before she could pull it back. "I'd camp right here if I could."

The clatter of dishes from the kitchen broke the prolonged moment, and they released each other. It was too hard to say goodbye, so Mary just stood silent and watched Sophie retreat into the gloaming, slipping into the woods and back toward her own home.

That night, Mary couldn't sleep. She lay in bed replaying the afternoon over and over. She tried to sleep. She wanted to dream. She wanted to have the same dream she'd been having, about the swings, because she knew this time it would be different. This time it wouldn't be her Toronto neighbor Brandy waiting for her there, it would be her remarkable Sophie. The more she tried to sleep, the further away it drifted. The sky was full of ink when she last looked at it, but all she could see was the abundance of stars.

On a whim, Mary jumped from her bed, stepped into her

house slippers, and took to the stairs. This new feeling in her chest pushed her forward with a kind of bravery or stupidity or whatever it was that love brought out in people. She paused at the bottom, and seeing the lights were all out and the house quiet, she rushed down the hallway and through the kitchen, then burst out into the yard.

There's something wonderful about the outside at night. It is more fully itself. It demands you be more fully yourself. Mary felt free and huge, and it was as if she could feel every muscle in her body at once. She clapped her hands over her mouth to keep in a joyous scream and turned in circles across the grass. If anyone had been looking out just then, they would have thought a ghost was dancing its way through the night.

Mary had to talk to someone right then, had to share all this great good that was filling her lungs every time she took a breath. She fell to her knees and found several small, loose stones in the scrub. Then she carefully marked the attic window and, closing one eye, aimed as best she could, letting the first one fly. It missed by a short distance, bouncing off the shutters. She recalibrated and tossed the second. This one clanked off the glass and fell back near her feet. She let go of the third—

There was movement in the window—the curtains being drawn back, and there stood her beloved Olive, who looked a bit scared by the unexpected noise. Mary jumped up and down, waving her arms in the air until Olive found her and smiled. The girl waved down, looking well in her excitement.

On instinct, and not knowing she was going to do it before it began, she dropped to one knee, and only moving her mouth with no volume that would wake an unintended audience, she began to recite—

*"But, soft! what light through yonder window breaks?*
*It is the east, and Juliet is the sun."*

Olive laughed, covering her mouth. She clapped, then kept her hands clasped to her bosom, hamming it up as if she were really Juliet and Mary Romeo on the lawn.

*"Arise, fair sun, and kill the envious moon,*
*Who is already sick and pale with grief."*

Then, to let her know she had also been reading, Olive mimicked the next verse back so that the two girls, one in the window of a locked room and the other a specter in a white dressing gown in the night, were mouthing a love story to each other.

*"That thou her maid art far more fair than she:*
*Be not her maid, since she is envious;*
*Her vestal livery is but sick and green*
*And none but fools do wear it; cast it off.*
*It is my lady, O, it is my love!*
*O, that she knew she were!"*

A dog began to bark from somewhere nearby, and the spell was broken. Mary stood, took a deep bow, and dashed back into the house, up the stairs and into her bed. She fell asleep with a smile on her face.

---

The next morning, Mary awoke to movement in the hallway. She stretched out until her feet and hands reached the corners of the bed. The sun was already up—she had slept later than usual, and it poured warm and bright into her room, onto her skin. And then she remembered—all of it, and the memory made her contract like a night flower. She held herself in the center of her bed, arms wrapped around her knees, chin to her chest. She tried to hold it there, the ball of excitement that settled in the cradle of her ribs.

She had been kissed. She had been kissed by *Sophie*!

There was banging from down the stairs like things being moved. She threw the blankets off and pulled on a simple cotton dress. She would do her hair later, before Thomas showed up. She was lacing up her shoe when the front door slammed shut. She paused. That sharp *bang* changed the air in the house. Suddenly the space felt smaller. She straightened up and whispered her thought out loud. "Uncle Craven?"

She took off running, into the hall and down the stairs. Was he really home? Was this it, the end of the torturous wait?

The end of Olive's solitary confinement? She tried to think of the words she would say, the ways she would convince him to release her cousin, who was clearly not deathly ill, just maybe a little weakened. The fresh air would do her good. Mary would be her constant companion.

She took the steps quickly, rehearsing her greeting in her head. The foyer was empty. Where would he have gone? She paused on the bottom step and listened. Someone cleared their throat—the parlor! She took stock of herself. Her hair was a mess, so she tried to pat it down into place. She checked the buttons on her dress and straightened out the skirts, then folded her hands demurely in front of her and walked into the parlor with her chin tilted and a smile on her face.

There was one person seated there, in front of the empty hearth, and it was not Uncle Craven.

"Good morning, Mary." Rebecca was very still, back straight, her eyes dark.

"Aunt Rebecca?" Even then, Mary's skin began to crawl. Something was wrong.

"I see your penmanship could use some work." And that's when Mary saw a letter—*her* letter—in Rebecca's lap. The envelope was open and the pages unfolded.

"You . . . You read my letter?" She couldn't think of anything more to say. She had never imagined this moment. It was too horrible to predict.

"Yes. The mail carrier came by this morning. It seems

Mr. Craven had left Michigan when it arrived and so they returned it to sender."

She had never before noticed how loud the grandfather clock ticked, but she did now. She counted eleven ticks from that clock before her aunt stood, holding the pages and letting the envelope fall to the ground.

Mary had the sudden urge to flee. She took a step back. "I need to . . . I should get ready for French le—"

"Mr. March will not be coming today, or any day. Lessons are canceled. Everything . . ." She made herself pause and take a breath. Her voice was getting loud. "Everything is canceled. Nothing will be the same now."

# 16

# Showdown

Mary spent a morning in her room volleying between weeping into her pillow and punching it as hard as she could. After she had calmly made her way up the stairs, shocked into obedience, Rebecca had come up. She didn't see her since she had closed her door behind her. But she heard her on the stairs and in the hallway, heard her pause on the other side of the door, and then heard the distinct *click* of a lock. She knew before she checked it that she was now a prisoner in her own quarters.

Mary paced in front of her window, watching the tree line, waiting for Sophie to arrive. Yesterday seemed so long ago now that she was on the other side of this terrible thing. Rebecca had read her letter. She knew the medicine was replaced. She knew they were trying to reach Olive's father. She knew enough now to keep her locked up in this room.

For a few minutes, Mary contemplated tying her bedsheets together and slithering out the window. She even pulled them off and tried to measure them by laying them end to end and then eyeballing the drop from her window. The house was tall and there would be some sort of drop to the lawn. She was willing to risk it, but she also wasn't sure the sheets would hold together. Besides, she reasoned, she couldn't just abandon Olive like that. She needed to stay and she needed to plan.

If worse came to worst, she thought about making a break for it when the door was unlocked for food delivery, as it was when she was sent up here before. Flora would let her out, and then she could sneak by her aunt if she were quiet enough. Finally, she decided that once Sophie showed up, she would make enough noise that Flora would be sent up, then she'd make a run for it, straight through the house and out the door. She would get the police to listen or find her uncle herself and make sure he returned and took care of Olive, and then she wouldn't come back until the whole thing was settled. Flora would be here to explain, and Philomene and even Jean could back her up. Yes, she needed to be free of her room, free of her aunt, and back with Sophie. That was the most crucial thing.

Once the plan was made, she dressed in her best escape outfit—her custom trousers, a white blouse, and the sturdiest shoes she owned. Fetching the shoes from the back of her closet, she touched the edge of her small suitcase, the one that had held her ribbons and books when she first arrived. She pulled it out.

Mary thought carefully about what she wanted to pack. She lay the empty case on her bed and carefully considered everything in her room. She packed a few changes of clothes—things that were practical and warm. Who knows where they would end up? Perhaps they would find safety in the north. At any rate it was best to be prepared. The warmer clothes took up most of the space, so she had room left for only one book, and she chose the volume about plants she had borrowed from her uncle's library. They would have to restart a garden when they found a place, if only to grow the things that would go on a plate with the fish and the deer Sophie would bring home.

When lunch didn't appear, she began to wonder if she would ever eat again. She also wondered if her chance at escape would ever materialize. No, she knew Flora wouldn't let her starve, and she wouldn't let her rot up here either. Instead of focusing on her empty stomach, she sat down to write. She wasn't sure what she would write, she just picked up the pen, dipped it in ink, and set the nib on the page. What came out was a letter to the one person she needed to talk to more than anyone right now.

*Mary,*

*Things look bleak, but you need to hold fast. Here is where you need to remember to be the biggest you can be. The letter was not delivered, so there is no one coming to save Olive. That means you have to find a way to do it. Maybe you can talk to Rebecca. Maybe she will understand, maybe even have gratitude. After all, you didn't exactly lay the blame at her feet. (Though, one could certainly have read it that way.)*

*And no, Sophie is not here yet, but perhaps she's waiting in the garden. Maybe she didn't want to come up to the house. Maybe even Flora got word back to her that today was not a good day to stop by. Maybe she knows you are locked up like Rapunzel with shorter hair.*

*As I write this, it occurs to me that perhaps Sophie went home, thought about the incident in the garden, and felt a great shame. After all, didn't Flora say the half-breeds are Catholic? The Catholic church surely would not understand a love like ours. Who would?*

*No. No, don't do that. Now there are tears on the page, and they'll smudge the ink. Mary, hold fast! And think!*

*You need to be ready to leave if that's what it comes to. But first, you need to try to set things right. The first place you should run, since you are preparing to do just that, is straight to Aunt Rebecca, to try to make her see you were only looking after Olive. After all, Olive is now her daughter and the only child she can claim. She should be grateful. Yes, remember that, she should, above all, have gratitude.*

*You can do this. You are big enough to make yourself small for this woman if it means protecting the two girls you love above all others.*

*Yours truly,*

Mary

She folded up the paper into the smallest shape it would hold and then pushed it into a wide crack in the floorboards. There was no use leaving more letters around to be read by the wrong eyes. And then she sat there, her chin resting in a cup made by her hands, elbows propped up on the desktop.

Birds visited the backyard, but none of them was a crow. A fox took its time meandering through the longer grass and was finally scared away by a porcupine, its ridiculous body lumbering by as if it were sightless and in a rush. But no girl. No Sophie. She tried to find Jean, but he wasn't out today. Her stomach grumbled and she moved to her bed. To pass the time, she fell into a dreamless sleep.

It was dark when she woke up. She lit a lamp and looked around, confused at first, disoriented. Her suitcase was still at the foot of the bed, her ink and paper out. But on her chair was a small plate and a glass cup. She took them both back to the bed and dug in. It was just water and two slabs of day-old bread with a thin layer of grease, but she ate it with relish and washed it down with the water in one gulp.

There was a small water closet attached to her room, so she was able to relieve herself and wash her face. She cleaned her teeth and brushed her hair and made a feeble attempt at braiding it. But not only was she too clumsy-fingered to pull it off, it only made her think of Sophie. And that's when the tears began. She cried as she cleaned up, put on her nightgown, and wrapped her soap to place in the suitcase. She cried at the window, watching the grounds shimmer under a close moon, and then she cried herself back to sleep. There was nothing more to do than this.

The next day, it rained. Not a light shower that watered the ground and misted your hair, but the heavy violent rain that came with great booms of thunder and angry slashes of light cutting through the sky. There would be no Sophie today.

Mary unpacked her book and read about every plant listed as medicinal, making careful notes on each. She took note of ideal soil conditions for different edible roots and included the proper growing seasons for all. Now she didn't need to take the book, which both prevented her from being a thief and opened up enough space in the case for another pair of shoes—her light ballet slippers that made her feel delicate.

Once again, when she woke from a nap, there was a small plate and a glass cup on her chair, but this time, she ignored them, turned over, and went back to sleep. Many hours passed in this way with not a single remembered dream to punctuate the wait.

On the third day, someone knocked politely at her door. Mary was standing in a patch of sunlight, her eyes closed, trying to remember what it felt like to be kissed. She opened her eyes and cleared her throat.

"Come in."

It was Philomene. Mary had never seen her on the second floor of the house before. She kept her eyes on the floor as if Mary were standing there in a dressing gown instead of her blue striped dress.

"Madame requests you for lunch," she said.

Mary opened her mouth to instruct her to go back downstairs and kindly tell Rebecca to go jump in the lake, preferably with her winter clothes on. But she knew she had to go. If she was going to have any opportunity to try to set this all right, this was it.

The walk to the dining room took forever in the eerily quiet house. Her hunger disappeared somewhere between the top of the stairs, when she had thought about Flora's homemade bread, and the bottom step, when she thought about having to face her aunt. She stalled in the foyer, and in those borrowed seconds, she tried to think of things she would say. But to do that, first she needed to sort out her feelings.

Fear was the one that demanded the most attention. It always was. It was the emotion that got in the way of all others, that was so loud, sometimes you thought it was everything. She was scared for Olive, for herself, for the freedom to see and spend time with Sophie. She was also anxious. How would this go, exactly? Was she expected to explain herself? Would she have to listen in silence?

But mostly, there was despair. Since despair was like smoke, it could coat everything. To feel despair was to see the world in new colors, or rather, one color—a kind of thick gray that left everything without nuance. Fingers had no prints, music had no swell or tremble, the sky had no stars. Despair made everything flat, and without the hope of her uncle receiving her letter, she was dangerously close to it. It seemed almost that despair was waiting just up ahead, through the dining room doorway.

She took a deep breath and stepped into the room.

"Sit," Rebecca instructed.

Mary took her usual seat and waited to be served. She was eager to see Flora after two full days being locked away. She tried to stay calm so she wouldn't launch into a full investigation on the whereabouts of Sophie.

"Make your own plate," Rebecca said without looking up from her own. "No one is going to wait on you, and you should get used to being a little more self-reliant, at any rate.

After all, in this world, you are the only person you can really ever fully trust. You've reminded me of that lesson, so I'm sure I should be thankful for that."

Mary didn't know how to respond. You're welcome, maybe? No, that wasn't right. She put some boiled carrots and a helping of peas on her plate instead. There wasn't much else on the table. So much for fresh bread. There wasn't even any meat or butter for the vegetables.

"Can you pass the salt, please?"

Rebecca ignored the request and kept talking as if Mary hadn't spoken at all. "You know, I began to think, a girl who would write a sneaky letter to my husband, that's the kind of girl who would do other sorts of sneaking around. So when I went up to the attic yesterday afternoon to check on poor Olive, who has been deprived of her medication for so long, I looked around to see what I could see. And you know what?" She looked up all of a sudden, her eyes like accusatory lights shone in Mary's face.

"What?"

"I didn't see anything." She looked back down, aggressively cutting her carrots into small bits with her fork and a butter knife, the silver scaping across the plate as the slimy vegetables jostled and slid.

Mary let herself feel a few seconds of relief. Thank God.

"Well, I didn't see anything at first, that is. But then, when I was turning the mattress, what do you think I found underneath it? Letters. Many more sneaky, snide, criminal letters." She slammed her cutlery down on the table, and Mary jumped.

Rebecca's chair scraped against the floor as she pushed it back and stood. She clasped her hands behind her back and walked to the large window overlooking the backyard. "In these letters, I discovered that not only had you been trespassing and breaking in to see Olive, but that you had accomplices in your treachery."

Now it was Mary's turn to glare. "What do you mean . . . ?" It came to her at once and she stood, shouting as she did, "Flora?"

There was no answer, but a thin young woman with a very pinched face wearing an old-fashioned bonnet rushed from the kitchen. "Did you need something then, luv?"

"Who are you? Where is Flora?" Mary practically shouted at the diminutive Englishwoman who looked to her employer for guidance.

"It's all right, Shelby. Go back to the kitchen." At that, the woman quickly scooted away.

"What did you do?" Mary smacked both hands down on the table, palms open. Now it was Rebecca who jumped.

"What did I do? Me?" Rebecca was made to play the victim; she did it so well. "You mean, what did *you* do to make this happen."

Of all the emotions Mary had shuffled through over the

past forty-eight hours, anger was not one of them, but here it was and it was huge, red, and sharp all over. This made it difficult to hold on to, and the best thing to do with it was to throw it. So she took aim at Rebecca.

"No, I mean you! We were all fine here before you showed up. I wish you would have stayed away!"

Rebecca met this with a smirk. "Says the orphan literally dropped on our doorstep."

"Yes, well, at least I'm not the conniving bitch who wormed her way into a wealthy marriage by convincing a man he needed her because his daughter was so ill. Especially since she was dead set on *keeping* her ill!"

Once she said it, so much became clear. Mary panted a bit, drawing big breaths, in and out. It was like there was suddenly so much room, and she didn't know what to do with it all.

Rebecca was able to take the first barb lightly, but this one hit her somewhere deep. Her mouth was a round O of shock.

Mary got a handle on herself and went back in. "Why else would you give her poison? I wanted to think it was a mistake, but it's clear the only mistake here is my uncle having married you!"

Rebecca took a few steps toward her, arms outstretched, and for a moment, it looked like she was going to grab her and give her a shake, but she composed herself. She took a sip of water, and the glass trembled in her grasp. "You don't even know what you're talking about."

"Yes I do."

"I tried. I gave her the medicine that would keep her calm, quiet. I tried."

"I don't believe you. And I can't wait to tell my uncle. He's going to throw you right out of the manor!"

That was the step too far—the statement that pushed Rebecca into survival mode, which was something she was used to. "Well, I can't see as to why he'd believe you. Olive was housebound before I came along. That girl hasn't been normal or healthy a day in her life. It's not my fault the nature of her illness changed over the years to where she is now. No. Nothing changed when I came, nothing much. But *everything* changed when you showed up. And here's the thing, sweetheart. Mr. Craven loves me. I am his wedded wife. You on the other hand? You are his brother's brat, a brother he never saw and didn't much care for to begin with. So ask yourself, who is he going to believe? Who is going to be thrown out?"

Mary didn't want to believe her, but everything was heightened and fast, and some of what she was saying made her feel like throwing up. "What's happened to Flora?"

"Well, dear, see, I actually have evidence, in your letters no less, of the backstabbing, scheming, and thievery that half-breed did in my house. So I let her go."

"You fired her?"

"Of course I did," Rebecca said, sitting back in her seat now that she had retaken the upper hand. "I would have gotten rid of Jean, too, but he seems to have disappeared on his own—unreliable bunch they are. Of course, I'll have to convince my husband to let Hippolyte go. I would myself, but he seems to have some sort of affection for the useless old man, and he's harmless enough for now . . ." She had trailed off, almost talking to herself, but she rallied back. "And I'm going to do more than that. You see, the constables will be here tomorrow morning so that I can file an official complaint and have them arrested."

Mary's heart felt like it nearly stopped. "Arrested? But you can't!"

"Oh, everyone knows those savages are no good in the house. No, they're meant for paddling your boat and selling you cheap meat, that's all. They can't be trusted." She sniffed, picked up her cutlery again, and forked a few musky peas into her mouth. "And don't think I've left out your little playmate either. No, no. That one will be dragged to a boarding school or a juvenile center for everything she did."

"Sophie?" It was barely a whisper.

"Stealing gardening tools, breaking in repeatedly to my home and my gardens. Ha! She'll be lucky if she ever sees these woods again." She dabbed at the corner of her mouth with a napkin. "How could you let her defile your family like that?"

Rebecca looked up, but there was no one in the dining room with her to answer. And when she got to the window, all there was to see was the green quilt of grass and leaves and a single flash of blue stripes pushing into the trees.

# 17

# Run Home

She hadn't stopped moving, hadn't begun thinking beyond a singular goal, until she got to the seventh garden. And now she was still, and her mind spun off in different directions like the skimmer bugs that skated across the surface of water.

The door was closed, and two planks of wood crossed it at a diagonal, hammered into the grout between the stones in the wall. She went to them now, pulling and trying to dig at the grout. When it was clear they would hold fast no matter what she did, she took off again. Besides, she wasn't looking for the garden right now, she was looking for a girl.

The lake was loud today, the wind leftover from yesterday's storm having whipped waves to roll. They fell on the shoreline again and again, pushing the wet line up the sand to almost where the rocks and weeds began. Mary was glad it wasn't calm. That wouldn't have made sense right now. Shading her eyes, she scanned the perimeter—nothing. Not even a single fisherman on an outcropping, not a boat on the horizon. She ran off, eyes wide, panting with the pace.

The clearing for the abandoned house Sophie called the Old Fort was still. A flock of small birds swirled from one side of the woods, across the plain like an unspooling ribbon, and back into the woods on the other side. Mary turned in a full circle, breathing hard, holding her stomach as if she would fall apart without hands there to keep her together.

Sophie emerged from the doorless gap in the house. "Mary? Mary, what's wrong?"

Hearing her voice brought Mary to her knees. She didn't know she had started crying until Sophie was cradling her, wiping away the tears.

"It's over," she sobbed. "It's all over."

---

The afternoon was sliding toward evening, and she was no longer jumping at every branch snap or animal movement. They were lying on the stage in the back of the house. Sophie had gone inside and retrieved what she called her "day pack," the supplies she brought with her when she was wandering. She laid out a wool blanket with wide stripes on the wood and instructed Mary to sit. Then she served them both tea from a metal thermos and smoked fish and scone that had been wrapped in a thin tea towel.

Mary hadn't eaten very much in the last few days, and her hunger returned with muscle. She devoured her food and half the thermos before she'd even begun to explain what was going on. Sophie waited patiently, sipping at her tea straight from the canister.

"So now, what's over?"

Mary started. "Rebecca got my uncle's letter. It was returned."

"I know."

Mary was shocked. "You know?"

"Of course." She shrugged. "You think Flora comes home madder than hell and spitting fire in the middle of the day all the time?"

"Oh . . . right." Mary felt foolish. Of course Sophie knew her sister had been fired over it. "I'm sorry, I'm being an ass. This has already affected you. How is she?"

"Don't be sorry, Jesus. Why d'you think I'm out here? Waiting to see if you showed. We were all worried about you, locked up in that house with that woman." She clicked her tongue. "I been watching when I could, tryna see you in a window, watching for that demon to see what she's up to."

"Wait, you were at the manor?"

Sophie searched her face with her eyes. "Are you serious? Of course I was."

Mary felt such gratitude, such relief. She had never been alone, not for one minute of it. She leaned forward and planted a small, grateful kiss on Sophie's mouth. It was so quick, there was no time to respond. When she'd moved back, Sophie placed two fingers on her own lips, as if putting a lid on a pot to keep the contents inside.

"Oh God," Mary groaned. "Oh good God."

"What is it?"

Mary felt like she might throw up all the good food she'd just had. She reached over and grasped both of Sophie's shoulders. "Sophie, have the constables been to your house?"

"The police? Non. Why would they be there?" A small panic made its way onto her face.

"Because Rebecca is meeting with them. She's . . . she's telling them that you and Flora were stealing from her."

Sophie was up in a flash, swearing and shouting in her rapid-fire dialect. She paced the perimeter of the wooden platform, throwing her arms up now and then. Finally she turned. "We are no thieves!"

"Of course not, I know." Mary stood. "I'll go back, I'll explain. They have to listen."

"They won't have to do nothing." Sophie rubbed her forehead as if trying to clear her head manually. "That ole bitch, le ponce, she'll tell them you're mad, or lying. If she even lets you close enough to talk."

"So then, what do we do?"

Sophie took a deep breath and let it out slowly. "When are they coming? The policemen?"

"Tomorrow morning."

"Then tonight, we stay together."

---

They thought it was safer if Mary stayed hidden for now. A white girl "missing" in the woods was bound to attract attention—if Rebecca had even bothered to raise the alarm, which they weren't certain she would. She might just count her blessings and hope for a bear attack. But still, they had to be smart about this. So Mary stayed at the fort while Sophie ran home to tell Flora about the police.

She was gone for a few hours. During her absence, Mary tried to be useful. She used a cedar bough to sweep out the dilapidated house. There was a solid enough table in there, and she cleaned it as best she could with the tea towel from their bread. She used a canning jar she found in the corner as a vase for wildflowers she picked. There were no chairs, but there were two tree stumps brought inside to act as such, and though the heights were different, they would have to do. Once the dining area was as set as she could get it, Mary started to feel like maybe this was a place a person could live. Certainly not in the winter, though if anyone knew how to make it livable, it was Sophie.

The windows were paneless, so she found fresh cedar and hung them over the holes like lacy drapes, finding splits and nooks in the wood to secure them. "Might keep the bugs away," she thought out loud.

Aside from the table, there was only one other spot that could be improved. The space was small and the floor was flattened dirt, but in one corner, someone—probably Sophie—had laid down a large hide. Mary had never seen hide like this. She'd worn leather and had sat on furniture made of animal skins, but this was different. It was uneven in shape, and she spent a few minutes trying to imagine what animal it had come from. Then she carefully folded the blanket from the platform and placed it at the top of the hide, like one long pillow. Only then did she really consider that she would be spending the night with Sophie. Her stomach pulled itself together in intricate knots, and she set about clearing spiderwebs with a stick as a distraction.

Sophie returned with two satchels, one slung over each shoulder. She also had a fishing pole and a knife at her belt. Mary was waiting for her, perched on one of the stump seats.

"Well, that was a mess, holy."

Mary, suddenly nervous, wrung her hands together. "How so?"

"Well, Maman was in tears over it all. Flora was madder than hell, her. And the kids, well, they just wanted to come with me. I had to sneak away."

"So what are they going to do?"

Sophie dropped the bags on the table and looked around. "Étonnante! It looks good in here."

"Are they going to hide? Maybe they should come here."

Sophie was unpacking the first bag—a half dozen candles, another blanket, the thermos refilled. "No, hide where? Too many kids. It'd be like moving a circus, that." She had more smoked fish, dried out and wrapped in a cloth. Then she placed the empty bag on the ground and started on the second, which was mostly fishing gear and a loaf of bread.

"But what if they get arrested?" An image of Flora in the back of a paddy wagon sprung to Mary's mind. "You have to tell them to run!"

Sophie stopped fussing with their supplies, pulled to Mary's frantic tone. "Listen, cherie. Us? We are used to being hauled in for every little thing. Something goes missing, someone gets hurt, any kind of mischief, they come across the Bay before looking at themselves. Flora is tough. She says they don't take you right away, them. They ask questions and look around and then they come back. There might be time to wait for Monsieur Craven to come and sort it."

Mary was crying again, but this time without sound. Just

tears plopping onto her dress. "But what if he doesn't come? The letter came back. He doesn't even know."

"If it is bad, Flora will find a way out west before they take her. Maman, her family are Dusomes, and they came from the Red River. Flora can find a way there if she has to. Don't worry. And if it comes down to it, well, I can, too." She sounded confident until the last bit, and when Mary looked up, she caught Sophie wiping at her eyes.

They tried to stay busy playing house. It was too late to go fishing, so they organized the nets and hooks for the morning. Sophie told her stories of her Père, and Mary shared a sad tale of her passing out at a Christmas party, much to her parents' indignation. They laughed as much as they could. That sound pushed the fear and darkness out of the little shed. Then they lit the candles and sat down at their table to eat a plain dinner that tasted like a royal banquet to them.

When it was time for bed, they took their shoes off and lay down in their clothes on top of the hide.

"You want to take this one?" Sophie grabbed the edge of the folded blanket Mary had placed. "I have another, too. Which one do you want?"

Mary looked away when she answered. "I need a pillow, or I won't fall asleep. Can we just . . . leave it? We can share the one you brought."

Sophie moved quietly, like she did when she was trying to

not scare a rabbit in the bush. She left the blanket by their heads and spread the other over Mary. Then she took off her jacket, pulled her suspenders off her shoulders so that they hung at her waist, and crawled in beside her.

The blanket wasn't big, so they lay pressed against each other, staring up at the ceiling. It was then that Mary noticed there was a hole in the roof. Crickets sang in the woods all around. A full moon made the sky navy and the few candles they left burning created a kind of halo in the corner.

"Hope it doesn't rain," Mary said.

"No rain tonight." Sophie's voice was deeper when she whispered.

Mary swallowed and closed her eyes to speak, like seeing and hearing at this moment was one thing too many.

"Sophie?"

"Yes?"

"Can you kiss me good night?"

She heard Sophie release her breath with a bit of a hitch as she moved onto her side. The blanket shifted across her legs, leaving behind a trail of goose bumps. Sophie's hand was placed carefully on her stomach, and Mary felt her blood pool there just under her skin. It was warm. She wanted that warmth to be everywhere all at once. There was a pause, and when Mary opened her eyes, she saw Sophie, framed by the sky through the roof above them, her head bowed, her eyes narrowed. Then their lips touched, and everything but this slight connection went away. Mary moved in closer and Sophie responded by curving her body over top. The kiss went on forever, for a moment, for a lifetime. Sophie's hands were in her hair, on her neck, moving across her stomach, fingers counting her ribs.

And when they fell asleep, two girls braided together on the edge of the Bay, it was the most beautiful sight in the woods. The lake understood that something monumental had occurred, and the crickets played a symphony to the union. It was a small miracle, the kind that only girls can create, and for now, it was everything in the whole universe.

But in the end, there were only a few stars, through a hole in the roof, as witness.

# 18

# Some Shall Be Pardoned, and Some Punished

MARY KNEW EXACTLY WHAT SHE HAD TO DO WHEN SHE WOKE UP. Sophie had left early to try her luck at fishing. She had a few traps in the area she was going to check, too. But Mary had a different chore to take care of.

Sophie was right; no one was going to listen to Flora or Philomene or any of them. No one would believe them over Rebecca. And her uncle was still gone, so she couldn't rely on him. But there was one person who could speak up, that would make them listen, and it was her. She was an English girl from the city *and* she was a Craven to boot. What was the point of having status in this society if you weren't going to use it to stand up?

So after Sophie left, she laced up her shoes, and without looking back—it would have been too painful to look back—she set off, back to the manor.

The walk back was the shortest it had ever been.

*When you don't want to be somewhere, it comes too soon*, her mother had said in their carriage once. They had been on the way home at the time.

Mary tried to stretch it out like she had on her walk into the dining room the day before—had that really just been the day before? It seemed like a lifetime ago. She stopped down at the shore and attempted to skip rocks. They only sunk with a comical *plunk*.

Passing the garden was bittersweet. She wondered when they would be able to return to it. Once she explained herself and cleared up this whole mess, she would still have to live with Rebecca, and she wasn't sure how easy that would be. Maybe she could remove the wood herself. Maybe she and Sophie could meet in secret. She walked past her locked haven and up the path, then cut into her yard.

From back here, it was impossible to know what was going on inside. She remembered Sophie telling her she had come for her, that she had skulked around the property trying to see her.

"So she was Romeo, after all," Mary said, smiling at the thought. Oh, that would piss her off. She would tell her when she went back to the fort.

Thoughts of Sophie on her mind, Mary squared her shoulders and walked confidently across the grass toward the manor. The back door was unlocked and she walked inside. Rebecca's new girl, Shelby, gawked.

"Oh, miss, you are in some kind of trouble, I'd say."

"Thank you, Shelby. But I don't need your insight right now." She crossed the room and started up the hall.

Two police officers stood in the foyer, speaking quietly to Rebecca. At her aunt's feet was a pile of old clothing, castoffs that had been set aside to be salvaged for the fabric that could be repurposed. As she came closer, Mary caught a bit of what Rebecca was saying.

"I found this in her quarters. Seems she had been stealing things quietly, for goodness knows how long—"

"Wait, what?"

Suddenly, all eyes were on her.

"Mary! You're back, thank goodness—" Rebecca took a step in her direction.

"Where did you get that?" Mary cut her off, pointing to the clothes.

Rebecca clasped her hands together and sucked in her cheeks a bit, trying to look serious and hurt. "Sadly, we found this in the maid's room. Flora is a thief, Mary."

"She's not a thief." Mary crossed the foyer quickly and rustled through the pile. "These are old things, things you were going to throw out. I asked her to put them aside for our play."

"Play?" The older officer had an Irish accent and a white mustache and was obviously the one in charge. "What's that you're talking about, miss?"

"A play," she repeated. "*Romeo and Juliet*. We were going to put on a production."

"And who's we, now?" he asked.

"Myself and Sophie—"

"Ah yes," Rebecca jumped back in. "And then there is the matter of the vagabond from down the basin. Sophie is Flora's sibling, I believe, though who can keep track of these huge families? They multiply like cats." She wrinkled her nose. "Anyway, that particular Beausoleil had been stealing garden supplies."

"You shut up!" Mary turned on her, vicious and quick. "Don't say another bad thing about her or—"

The younger officer stepped in between them, his shadow falling over Mary. "Or what, miss?"

"Ugh, now do you see what I've been dealing with here? Robbed by Indians, a sickly child to care for, and an orphan with an obvious illness of the head." Rebecca threw her hands up and gave a great impression of a woman on the verge of collapse. "I mean, I can't completely blame her. After all, she did just lose her parents. And I was only trying to do my Christian duty."

"I am not lying!" Mary was growing frantic. But even so, she heard what she must sound like, and it was a lot like the picture Rebecca was painting. "No! I'm not sick and I'm not lying. You have to believe me."

The two officers were silent, and in that silence, a man coughed from the parlor. Mary looked in, but she didn't recognize him. He was slight and balding and wearing a badly wrinkled linen suit. He was leaning against the hearth, regarding her with some curiosity.

"I have a nun arriving the day after tomorrow from Saint Jude's in Montreal," Rebecca continued. "It's a school for troubled girls run by the church. I was planning on having her rest here until the carriage arrived, but I can see now that perhaps it's best you take her in hand until then. She's already run away once."

"She's been poisoning my cousin. Go see for yourself!" Mary shouted.

"Gentlemen, I am Dr. Stuart." The strange man came forward now, shaking hands with both officers. "I am Olive Craven's physician, and I can attest to the well-being of the girl. She remains, of course, in the throes of her lifelong affliction, poor wretch, but she has, and I cannot stress this enough, not been poisoned, either accidentally or with malice."

He chuckled a bit to indicate the absurdity of the claim.

"In fact, Mrs. Craven has been an excellent caregiver over these years—"

"Don't you mean *your sister*?" Mary interjected. "How can you be expected to tell the truth against your own sister?"

The older officer raised his bushy eyebrows. "Is this true, Doctor? Are you and Mrs. Craven related?"

"Yes, Sergeant, it is a fact that Rebecca and I are family. However, I was Olive Craven's doctor before she met and subsequently married Mr. Craven. In fact, it was on one of my visits she was assisting at that they met. I'd like to take credit for that and perhaps be remembered fondly in their will." He laughed and the rest of the adults joined in.

"How can you believe him? How can you be making jokes at a time like this?" Mary was screaming now. "He should have stopped her. He knew better. Arrest her! Arrest them both!"

The doctor and the sergeant exchanged a quick look between them, then the older man sighed. "Listen, lassie. No one is being arrested here today, not in this house anyway. And if you don't calm down, we'll have to do as Mrs. Craven says and place you into custody until you're off to the convent."

Mary gaped, opening and closing her mouth like a fish out of water. How could it have come to all this? How could everything have crumbled so fast? The circle of adults around her was too much, all those eyes looking at her like she were a madwoman. Not one ally in the bunch. And now they wanted to take her away?

*Sophie.*

It was that single thought that started her moving, and she went with it. She had to get back to Sophie, to the fort, to their home. She couldn't go, not now, not when the nuns showed up—she wouldn't. She had to get out of here.

She bolted, pushing past Rebecca and knocking her over so that she yelped both out of surprise and pain.

"Stop!" The officers were yelling at her, but she had a head start. She was almost to the kitchen, and beyond that, she could see the back door, still open from when she had come in. She focused on the sun outside, the green expanse, freedom—

And then she collided with something. There was a clatter of pans and a shattering of crockery, and she was splayed out on the floor beside Shelby, all the wind knocked out of her body. She tried to find the door again, even from the kitchen tiles, but instead, the shadow of two men blocked out all the light.

They picked her up, an arm under each of hers, and marched her back up the hallway. The good doctor had collected his sister from the floor and seated her on a low bench by her ridiculous portrait.

"Take her out of here!" Rebecca cried. "I don't want her in my house for another minute!"

Mary hung her head. All her limbs were limp, and she was still trying to get her breath back, but even so, she was being escorted to the front door.

"Should I give her something for the ride? I have a shot that will calm her down," she heard the doctor say.

"If you think that best," the sergeant replied.

Mary closed her eyes. It was really all over.

Then the front door opened, and a new voice cut through the space.

"What is the meaning of all this?"

She opened her eyes and lifted her head. And there, striding in with Jean, was a tall man with a serious face, larger than life and already angry. She would have recognized him anywhere—he looked so much like her own father. "Uncle Craven?"

"Jean?" He motioned him forward, and Jean picked up Mary in one scoop. The officers did not resist.

"Mr. Craven, sir." It was clear he commanded a lot of respect by the way he was addressed. "We were called here by your wife."

"Yes." He shot a quick glance in Rebecca's direction, and she whimpered from her bench. "Jean came to find me and filled me in on what's been going on around here. I believe a larger conversation will need to be had."

"Darling, I can explain," Rebecca said.

"No." He held his hand out without looking at her. "I want to hear from my niece first."

Mary held on to Jean by the front of his shirt, and cradled

there, she felt for the first time like perhaps, someone might actually listen.

---

Flora was summoned back to the manor to oversee the packing of Rebecca Craven's things. It was probably the happiest day of her employment. She opened all the windows and sang while she folded dresses and rolled crinoline. Despite Mrs. Craven sitting in the back of her carriage the entire time, her life was carefully excised from the remaining habitants of the manor. Flora took her time. She wouldn't give Rebecca the satisfaction of calling her work sloppy now. No, she would arrive at her sister's with carefully packed crates, the fabric given exact creases and the fragile things safely wrapped.

"No, no, Jean, that set was Hattie's." She stopped the man from taking down a china tea set from the hutch in the dining room. "That stays here for the new little mistress of the house. But I know something I will need your help with."

She led him to the foyer and pointed to the portrait hanging near the stairs. He regarded it for a moment, squinting. "Who's that?"

"A witch, Jean," Flora replied, moving to grab one side. "Now help me banish her once and for all."

While the moving was well underway, William Craven

stood in front of the attic door. Behind him, Mary put a hand on his back. "We'll go together."

He fit the key into the lock, and with a deep breath, pushed the door open.

"Father!" Olive leapt from her bed and ran across the creaking attic. William collapsed to his knees. It was truly a collapse—there was no hesitation or grace in the movement, and Olive ran directly into his arms.

For a brief moment, Mary felt jealousy creeping under her skin. She felt the way all children who have been denied love feel when faced with it—hungry. She was starving, her stomach twisting up on itself until she closed her eyes and the image of Sophie appeared on her lids. No, she knew love. She had love, as much as anyone can have it. She had someone who reminded her that the fault was not hers, that the absence of love is sometimes what happens when you're living in a small world with other hungry souls, ones incapable of giving what they cannot recognize.

"Oh, my girl." William held Olive back for a moment, his eyes taking in her flushed cheeks, her wild hair, her big smile. "You look so well. You look . . . so much like your mother."

Olive's smile faltered and she pulled back out of his grasp. "But I am not her, Father. I am me and I am not a ghost."

"I know, sweet Olive. I know this. I always did, it was just . . . hard." His face crumpled. "I am so sorry—"

"Why?" she asked, interrupting his apology. "Why did you leave me here? With *her*?"

"I didn't know." He stood, arms still outstretched toward the girl, the emptiness of them seeming to hurt him. "I thought you needed a mother above all else, above my feelings, above my doubts. I thought I was doing right by you."

"I didn't need a mother. I just needed a parent." Now that she had started, Olive let all her anger bubble to the surface. She raised her voice. "I just needed you!"

Mary was the one who felt like a ghost now. She was pretty sure they had forgotten she was there, and she moved a step back into the shadows to allow them the intimacy that this moment demanded.

"I didn't know she was hurting you. The doctor . . ." William Craven passed a hand through his graying hair, sighing. "It doesn't matter what I thought. You were hurting, and I wasn't here because of my own damn grief."

Olive allowed him to feel small for a moment, and then she reached out and took one of his hands. "I grieved, too, Father. I may not have spent time with my mother, but that doesn't mean I didn't feel the loss of her."

William pulled her to him through that small connection of hands and then held her face. "I will never leave again, never leave you by yourself."

Olive smiled again. "I don't need you by me every moment,

Father. I have Mary now and Sophie and everyone else. I just need to know that you are close by, if I should need you."

She embraced him, and he seemed to bend and mold his large body to that gesture. "Agreed. Always."

After a moment, the three of them made their ways down the steep steps and out onto the landing. At the bottom, Olive closed the door behind them and sighed. "I feel like Rapunzel finally returned from exile."

"And the prince saved you!" Mary added.

"No, Mary." Olive grasped her hand as they walked down the hall. "You did."

# 19

# A Garden for Three

ONE YEAR LATER

THE CROWD THAT HAD GATHERED AFTER THE WEDDING AWAITED the start of the production.

Flora was patient with her siblings, who buzzed around her like bees to a delicate, white lace flower. She gave each girl a flower from her bouquet to hold and saved a dance for each of her brothers. Their mother cried through the vows and insisted on working in the kitchen with her favorite cousin, Philomene, for much of the afternoon. Together, they served the biggest feast the Bay had seen in years.

Many relatives had arrived with fresh butchered spring bear, iced fish, and baskets of baked scone for the meal. One aunt even came with a crate of jarred jam, and they used half of it as cake filler. Though they were kept company by hordes of people coming in and out of the kitchen so that it became, at one point, the unofficial heart of the party, both older women emerged from the food preparation when the sun went down to talk and sing under the abundance of stars.

The ceremony was held in the garden, the best garden of them all—the one locked up so many years ago after Olive's mother had died, the one Sophie had toiled over while listening to Mary prattle on about a play that ultimately didn't make much sense when you were surrounded by a family who loved you and a home where you belonged. Henrietta's Garden, her uncle called it, and Mary didn't mind. It seemed like the right name for such a tragically beautiful spot.

When the ceremony began, Jean walked Flora down the aisle while two young fiddle players provided the music. It took him a moment to put her hand in Thomas's, so the younger man leaned in and whispered to him in French, "I promise to take good care of her. She'd handle me if I didn't."

The reception was joyous. Even Mr. Craven joined in the revelry, though not at the volume and enthusiasm of Flora's community. The March family made a brief appearance and then quickly returned to the town on the other side of this magical Bay, scared off by the laughter and fiddles of the half-breeds.

The house had been festooned with cedar boughs and floral arrangements. There was an impressive swag of roses draped over Henrietta Beausoleil's portrait, which had been reinstated to its place of honor in the foyer the day after Rebecca Craven moved out. Lanterns had been hung from the trees and set along the perimeter of the yard. They had been placed at even intervals down the path through the trees and into the garden, in case the ceremony had run late, which it did not. As much as everyone wanted to witness the union, they wanted to celebrate it even more and had made their way back toward the manor in good time.

It was the end of a chilly night with summer right around the corner, almost exactly one year since Mary had arrived from the city. The newly formed Craven family had been left with time and space to heal over the fall and winter. A specialist had been brought in from New York, who explained that what Olive suffered from was a common enough affliction of the nerves, where she felt a kind of panic at being out of her comfort areas. He explained it like the feeling you get when something bad happens—the way your whole body tenses and your mind spins, but that for Olive, it could happen without the bad thing. They learned ways to make her more comfortable and practiced breathing evenly when the nerves took hold.

After many months, the Cravens learned how to be a family of three with the support of their beloved household staff, including Sophie, who was being trained by Jean as the new gardener under his supervision. And at the beginning of spring, the Cravens were asked to host the wedding just weeks after Mr. March had proposed. It was Mary who answered on their behalf before her uncle even had the chance to fully understand the request.

"Oh yes, a thousand times yes! Of course we'll host! After all, Flora, you are a part of this family. The manor just wouldn't be the same without you, even on your wedding day. Oh, and we can put on our play in honor of the union!"

Then she grabbed up Olive from the couch, and the girls laughed and spun each other in dizzying circles around the parlor. "We'll sew new costumes, set lanterns in the trees, oh, it'll be like a fancy opening night!"

Seeing his only daughter laugh and move with such ease brought a light to Mr. Craven's face, and he watched with an indulgent smile. Philomene had leaned down near his ear. "Yes, she looks like Hattie, especially when she laughs, eh?"

And so it was decided. Mary had her and Olive and Sophie in charge of executing Flora's plans, which were much too humble for her liking. So she had petitioned her uncle for extras.

"Uncle, you know Flora was really instrumental in Olive's recovery. Without her, who knows what could have happened while you were gone." She nudged her cousin with her shoulder.

"Oh yes," she gave a small, practiced cough. "I was so

alone and near death, Father. I feel weak just remembering it all. If not for Flora, well . . ."

"Enough, you absolute conmen," Craven interrupted, raising his large hand at the dinner table to stop the performance. "Go and order your extra flowers and chairs. We will have champagne and a small cake brought in, but I put my foot down at a white carriage, and we are not building a dance platform, for the love of God. So just take those thoughts out of your heads."

On the evening of the wedding, before they left in their carriage for Collingwood and after they had cut their four-tier cake, Thomas and Flora sat in the front row while the girls debuted the play they had written themselves. It was held on that platform they'd convinced William to have constructed.

"This is the story of a girl trapped in a tower by an evil witch, but one whose hair wouldn't grow long enough to use as a rope." They'd employed Sophie's brother Louis to narrate, and he took his job seriously, carefully enunciating every word. "It's a story about a girl who didn't need a prince. Instead, she needed a poem."

Refusing to play the role of the captive again, Olive instead was the brave poet who recited poems to the girl in the tower, played by a swooning Mary draped in layers of pink petticoats. "O brave poet, keep watering the gardens with your rhymes. I can feel the earth shifting."

*"The walls of hate are tall and steep*
*Bricks laid down to make you weep.*
*I send these words on wings of dove*
*And crumble walls with signs of love."*

Louis and his brothers moved around the props, shaking the cardboard walls so that it looked like an earthquake had hit the ground. The men, already on their second glasses of cherry wine, cheered.

Sophie appeared as a wicked goblin who stole the pages of the poet while she slept. The men booed at this part. And when she awoke, the poet sobbed. "I've lost all my weaponry!"

"Be not afraid, kind poet, for the words were always only in your heart," Mary's character called out. And the poet, working through their nerves and doubt in a long, meandering soliloquy, finally delivered the winning blow:

*"You belong not in tower away and above,*
*You should be held with care and love.*
*Not in a cell up in the sky*
*Not spending days wondering why.*
*I call you down into all the rooms*
*Now, climb the vines of these Bay Blooms!"*

And with that, the boys collapsed the walls, and in their place, a trellis of bright red roses was hoisted. The audience went wild when Mary stepped onto the stage and into the arms of the poet and Sophie's goblin ran off the stage, shrieking. The half-breeds cheered, some shooting guns into the sky. Even William applauded from his spot at the back of the audience, behind the last row of chairs laid out on the lawn.

After accepting their accolades and sharing in the wedding cake, Mary found herself watching the riotous dancing from the back step, where Sophie found her.

"Hey, Madame," Sophie said in jest, bowing deeply at the waist. "Can I escort you to the garden where I toil endlessly?"

"Sophie, stop it with the madame merde." Mary gave the girl a slight push. "I am most certainly not the lady of the house and you are not *my* gardener."

"That's not true," she answered, straightening up to her full height. "I would hope that I am your everything."

Mary blushed as she stood and took the arm that was being offered. Sophie looked magnificent that day; she wore long, pale blue skirts with red petticoats that peeked out the bottom around her flat leather boots when she walked. She wore it with a black dress shirt, a dark tailored coat, and a small red ribbon tied around her neck. Her hair was braided as usual, though it was much longer now, the braids reaching to her waist and wrapped with pale leather strings. On the top of her head was perched the beaver top hat Mr. Craven had gifted her for Christmas. Together they walked down the lit path, through the trees, and followed the familiar and well-tread path to the seventh garden.

It was beautiful in here, more so than the year before and even now, before summer's humidity had the chance to close every green knot tight with sudden, lush growth. The garden was a special place for them; it was the place that had truly brought them together, the spot where they had found each other and themselves, and it was here where they still spent most of their time, understanding that not many others could begin to understand the way they felt. It was safe and beyond that, or perhaps because of that precisely, it was magical.

"Hey, there you are," Olive called from under the canopy of the willow. "I've been waiting."

She put her cat down, an old tom with one ear and a bad attitude for everyone but Olive. Sophie had brought him to the manor at the start of winter after finding him at the Old Fort. That day, he'd scratched and growled until Olive gathered him up in her arms, and there he remained as long as she would hold him. She named him Sweetie and the irony—to everyone but Olive, who was thoroughly in love—was endearing.

There were lanterns hung from the branches and some along the wall, with a few set on the rocks that curved like perfect seats from the ground. It was as if the stars had fallen just for the chance to be in the garden with these girls who the wild had allowed as curators of its beauty. Sophie's crow was quiet, but cautiously kept an eye on all this contained fire from his perch by the front gate as the girls dipped under the willow and nestled onto their swings.

There were three of them now, hung at even intervals, reinforced, and the splinters sanded out by Jean's own hands. They took a moment to get settled, looking at each other in their secret space, eyes lit to gemstones in the lantern light.

"Ready?" Olive asked, her cat settling in a mossy patch to watch.

"Ready," they answered in unison.

Then they pulled themselves back, pumped their legs, and on the momentum of their own muscles, broke through the barriers and sailed into the bright open with every star as witness.

# Acknowledgments

I am so grateful to Feiwel & Friends, in particular to Emily Settle and her amazing team, for the opportunity to reimagine *The Secret Garden*. I lifted the original story and placed it in my home community of Penetanguishene, Ontario. The early and ongoing Métis community seemed the perfect place for this story of love and struggle. We're good at both. Besides bringing the story to Indigenous territory, I wanted to write queer characters back onto the landscape in this time period. It's not "bold" or "new"; they have always been here.

My thanks to my brilliant agents, Rachel Letofsky and Dean Cooke, and the entire CookeMcDermid crew. And a special thank you to my family—Shaun, Jaycob, Wenzdae, and Lydea, thank you for giving me a beautiful home in my community in which to do this exciting work.

## AVAILABLE FROM REMIXED CLASSICS

**The sea and those who sail it are far more dangerous than the legends led them to believe . . .**

This remix of *Treasure Island* moves the classic pirate adventure story to the South China Sea in 1826, starring queer girls of color—one Chinese and one Vietnamese—as they hunt down the lost treasure of a legendary pirate queen.

**They will face first love, health struggles, heartbreak, and new horizons. But they will face it all together.**

In a lyrical celebration of Black love and sisterhood, this remix of *Little Women* takes the iconic March family and reimagines them as a family of Black women building a home and future for themselves in the Freedpeople's Colony of Roanoke Island in 1863.

Thank you for reading this Feiwel & Friends book.
The friends who made

# INTO THE BRIGHT OPEN

**A SECRET GARDEN REMIX** possible are:

Jean Feiwel, Publisher
Liz Szabla, VP, Associate Publisher
Rich Deas, Senior Creative Director
Anna Roberto, Executive Editor
Holly West, Senior Editor
Kat Brzozowski, Senior Editor
Dawn Ryan, Executive Managing Editor
Kim Waymer, Senior Production Manager
Emily Settle, Editor
Rachel Diebel, Editor
Foyinsi Adegbonmire, Editor
Brittany Groves, Assistant Editor
Samira Iravani, Associate Art Director
Avia Perez, Senior Production Editor

Follow us on Facebook or visit us online at mackids.com.
Our books are friends for life.